A Sleigh Bell Promise

By Marilyn Boone

A Sleigh Bell Promise
By Marilyn Boone

©2020 by Marilyn Boone

All rights reserved.
This book or parts thereof may not be reproduced in any form, stored in or introduced into a retrieval system, or transmitted, in any form, or by any means (electronic, mechanical, photocopying, recording, or otherwise) without prior written permission of the copyright owner and/or publisher of this book, except as provided by United States of America copyright law.

This book is a work of fiction. Names, characters, places, and incidents are a product of the author's imagination or are used fictitiously. Any resemblance to actual events, locales, or persons, living or dead, is coincidental.

Cover Design: Brandy Walker
    www.SisterSparrowGraphicDesign.com
Interior Design: Jennifer McMurrain
    www.LilyBearHouse.com

ISBN: 9798560299101

Also available in eBook publication

PRINTED IN THE UNITED STATES OF AMERICA

*This book is dedicated to all those who love the sleigh
bell, because those who do…
already love Christmas.*

Chapter One

Bethany glanced at her phone and breathed in a sigh of relief. She was only ten miles away from reaching her destination, a small town named Snow Valley. Though she usually didn't mind driving through the mountains, this trip was different. Just as fast as she could fulfill a promise to her mother, she would be hurrying back to the city where a packed suitcase and her boyfriend, Kenneth, were anxiously awaiting her return.

After a short stay with his parents, they would soon be spending Christmas together on the warm sparkling beaches of the Caribbean. Bethany couldn't help but dream something else would be sparkling before they returned home. What better way to commemorate their two years of dating, than for Kenneth to propose and place a diamond engagement ring on her finger.

"I still don't understand why you have to return this gift today, right before our trip. Why can't you wait until after the holidays?" Kenneth had questioned her before she left.

"Because I made a promise to my mother, and I'm sure you always want me to keep my promises," she posed, anticipating his response.

Kenneth wrapped his arms around her. "Of course, I do. Like the one you made that you'll love me forever."

Bethany looked up at him and smiled, "Yes, just like that one."

"And you're positive you don't want me to go with you?" His face expressed a hopefulness she would change her mind.

"It's not that I don't want you to," she answered, having to swallow a fair amount of guilt of being less than honest. "You have a report to finish for work, remember?"

Kenneth released his hold. "All right, I'll let you go, though you never did tell me what the gift was. It must be pretty important if you have to deliver it in person."

Bethany shrugged before opening the car door. "I only know it was important to my mother."

"Be careful then. My parents are expecting us for dinner at 7:00," he reminded her as she buckled herself in the seat and started the engine.

"Don't worry, I'll be back in plenty of time," she assured him, and with one last wave, she backed out of his driveway.

Bethany pulled onto the highway, chastising herself for not fulfilling the promise earlier. In the six months since her mother's funeral, launching the new fall line of Touché handbags followed by the ever earlier Christmas promotions had given her plenty of excuses for putting it off. That was until now, when her mother's final request could no longer be delayed.

Sitting beside her on that last day, Bethany watched her mother struggle to raise her weakened arm off the sofa and point toward the kitchen. "What is it, Mom?"

Her arm dropped as her voice strained to speak above a whisper. "The cookie jar…"

Bethany assumed there was something inside the jar her mother wanted. She rose from her chair to walk toward the kitchen, wondering what she might find stored in it this time. Despite what a cookie jar was intended for, she had her doubts it would be cookies. All the years she spent peeking and wishing, had taught her that. Except on rare occasions, the cookie jar's primary purpose was as a home to an assortment of coins, rubber bands, newspaper clippings and coupons.

Her mouth formed a wistful smile when she saw the owl shaped jar, occupying the same place on the counter it always had, between the refrigerator and the stove. Its large ceramic eyes gave it the appearance of the perfect watchman, even though the jar never held anything that needed guarding. Bethany was still curious, however, and removed the lid, surprised to see a small square box, sitting among the expected items. Lifting it out, she got a better look at its size and the shiny gold paper covering it.

Bethany returned to her mother's side with the box in her hand. "Is this what you were wanting?"

A peaceful calm swept over her face, temporarily transforming its pallor. "Besides you…it's the best gift I've ever received. Please, it needs to be returned by Christmas Eve."

Bethany stared into her mother's eyes that had since filled with moisture, causing hers to do the same. "I don't understand. Return this where?"

"Snow Valley," she said, then closed her eyes.

"Mom," Bethany cried out, fearful she was already gone, but as if her mother let go of the angel's hand for a brief moment, her eyes opened again and she sucked in another breath.

"The address is attached to the bottom of the gift. Promise me, Bethany…promise me you won't forget."

"I promise," Bethany said, watching her mother's eyes close for what would be the last time. "I love you, Mom," she added, praying her words weren't too late and her mother had heard them.

The memory brought fresh tears to Bethany's eyes. Unable to drive and rummage through her purse for a tissue, she fought back against letting them flow. She couldn't recall her mother ever asking for anything except for this one promise. Keeping it was the least she could do.

Bethany knew better than to have procrastinated, but there was no reason her plan shouldn't work. Three hours to Snow Valley, return the gift, then three hours back to the city. Her suitcase was already in Kenneth's trunk, packed and as ready as she was for the smells of sea salt and coconut scented sunscreen.

She hadn't been driving long outside the city before the scenery turned into tree covered mountains of birch and spruce. By then, the radio stations were mostly static, leaving Bethany a hostage to the quiet. If only her thoughts had remained quiet as well. Instead, they insisted on replaying Kenneth's remark that whatever was in the box must be something important. Bethany never considered unwrapping it to find out, so she could neither confirm nor deny his statement. It hadn't been hers to open, even though she never heard of returning a gift to its giver, much less by a certain day. In this case, Christmas Eve.

It was true, Bethany hadn't wanted Kenneth to come with her and was thankful he hadn't pressed her for more answers. If he knew what little information her mother had given her, he would have thought she was silly to be making such an effort right before their trip. Maybe she was. With all the medications her mother was taking, one might suspect the name and address weren't even real. Bethany chose to believe they were, but what mattered the most was she had made a promise and was keeping it.

Bethany maneuvered her car around another curve, grateful the sun was shining with hardly a cloud in the sky. There was also very little snow on the ground, which seemed odd for this time of year, especially considering the town's name. The sign for Route 20 was just up ahead, so she slowed down to exit the highway and soon found herself on a narrow two-lane road, seemingly leading nowhere. The same questions that popped into her mind while searching for the address began running through it again. *Why here? Why Snow Valley?* She had never even heard of this small town, much less been there.

Within another mile, she came upon a few houses scattered here and there until the road widened and was lined on either side with rows of small businesses, each one decorated with garlands and wreaths. She took a closer look, trying to decide the best one to stop in and ask for directions. While she had been able to find Snow Valley on the map, the street address wasn't showing up on any search. Surely, someone who lived here would know.

Joe's Country Store looked to be as good a place as any, so Bethany parked her car and got out, taking a minute to stretch her legs before opening the store's door. A loud jingling of bells announced her entry as she did.

"Welcome to Smithville. What can I do for you?" a man from behind the counter asked.

Bethany shook the ringing from her ears and looked at him with obvious confusion. "Smithville?"

Chapter Two

"You mean, Snow Valley? That's where my phone says I am." Bethany's response was replete with skepticism.

The man behind the counter glanced at another gentleman placing items on a shelf. "Did you hear that Joe? Her phone says she's in Snow Valley."

"Here, I'll show you." She placed the phone's screen in front of him. "See the red pin…it says Snow Valley right next to it."

"Well, I'll be. I suppose the pin can't be wrong now. Nor the *Welcome to Snow Valley* sign you must have missed, coming into town." He shook his head while grinning. "I'm afraid more people rely on their phones to tell them where they're going than looking with their own eyes."

"So, I *am* in Snow Valley." Bethany stated as if that were the only acceptable conclusion.

"I reckon you are after all," he said with a wink.

By then the other gentleman had walked over to join them. "You'll have to excuse, Joe, ma'am. We don't get many folks in here from out-of-town to poke a little fun with."

"Wait, didn't I just hear him call you, Joe?" Bethany's eyes shifted between them, calculating what she had heard. "Are you both named Joe?"

"Yes ma'am. I'm Joe, and he's Joe Jr.," the man behind the counter answered, pointing first to himself, and then to the man next to him. "No relation, mind you," he added.

As if having the same name wasn't confusing enough, it appeared they were very close to the same age. Though it may have made for an interesting conversation, Bethany resisted the temptation to ask any more questions than necessary. She was on a mission and couldn't risk becoming mired in any lengthy explanations she wasn't sure could even be believed. "Well, I have a question for you, Joe."

Both men looked at her. "Either one of you," she clarified with a contained sigh. This part of her trip was already taking longer than she had planned.

"I have a small package I need to deliver to someone. His name is…" she started while reaching into her pocket.

"Joe?" Joe Jr. grinned with a twinkle of mischief in his eyes.

Even Bethany couldn't help from joining in the laughter that followed. "No, his name isn't Joe."

She pulled out the address that was once attached to the gold wrapping. "It's a Nicholas Smith, Box 1, Oaktree Lane."

Joe's eyes softened. "You sure that's the right name?"

Bethany turned the piece of paper around so he could read her mother's handwriting for himself. "I'm kind of on a tight schedule, so I'd greatly appreciate it if you could tell me how to get there."

"Getting there is the easy part," Joe Jr. spoke up in a voice that had grown softer as well. "You go three more blocks down Route 20 to Oaktree Lane, turn right and don't stop until you come to the end of the road," he said, motioning with his arm.

"You'll know when you can't go any farther," Joe added.

"Thanks, it was nice meeting you Joe and Joe." Bethany nodded twice before spinning around and practically running toward the door.

Amidst the sound of the jingling bells, she missed hearing the, "But, ma'am," that immediately followed.

Back inside her car, Bethany repeated the directions to herself. They sounded easy and quick. Even allowing for several minutes to meet Nicholas and return the gift, she wouldn't have any trouble staying on schedule. Per their instructions, Bethany turned right on Oaktree Lane and kept going. Whoever Nicholas Smith was, at least she now knew for certain, he was a real person.

What was already a narrow road, became even narrower between the rows of trees, until as Joe said, she couldn't go any farther. To her left was a small wooden house she presumed belonged to Nicholas. Bethany frowned at how dark and abandoned it looked. Besides there being no lights on, there was no smoke coming out of the chimney, something unusual for this time of year. He didn't seem to be home, but she knew there was only one way to find out.

Bethany turned to park in front of the house, then stepped out of her car and onto the porch. She was disappointed but not surprised when she knocked and no one answered. "Mr. Smith," she called out, knocking a second time.

She peered into the window beside the door for any signs of occupancy, a coffee mug next to a chair, a newspaper, or any other evidence revealing a person's daily routine. There was nothing but a few pieces of dusty looking furniture scattered in a room that didn't look like it had been lived in for a long time.

Puzzled, yet desperate not to lose any more time, Bethany hurried around to the back of the house in case he had been outside and hadn't heard her. "Mr. Smith," she called out again to avoid her appearance startling him. There was still no sign of Nicholas, only a separate wooden building set back away from the house. She walked closer to get a better look.

Whatever the building was used for, it appeared to be as deserted as the house. Bethany knocked on its door anyway, just in case. No answer yet again. She dropped her shoulders in frustration, having to admit it wasn't his fault he didn't know she was coming to see him. Maybe he was simply running an errand.

A sudden draft of much colder air blew through the trees, causing Bethany to shiver. She hadn't dressed appropriately enough to be in the mountains for an extended period, but she was willing to wait a little longer. She headed back to her car to find some warmth and keep watch. Checking the time, Bethany determined she had fifteen minutes to spare. If he didn't show up by then, she had no other choice but to leave.

The wait was slow while Bethany's eyes kept being drawn to the gold box she had removed from her purse. She wanted to be the one to give it to Nicholas, to know he had received it by Christmas Eve. That was the only way to be sure her promise had been fulfilled and find out what was inside that was so important to her mother. Unfortunately, another glance at the clock let her know she had run out of time.

Bethany returned to the country store and walked straight up to the counter where Joe was still standing.

"Nicholas wasn't home. Do you know if he is out of town or how I can reach him?" she asked, probing for more information that might help her find him.

"Ma'am, he's more than just out of town," Joe answered.

"I wish you would have mentioned that earlier. Please don't tell me he's out of state, or worse, out of the country." Bethany felt herself close to begging.

"You left before Joe Jr. or I could explain," Joe responded with gentleness. "The truth is he is none of those. I'm sorry to be the one to tell you, but Nicholas left this earth about five years ago."

"Left? This earth?" Bethany leaned on the counter while her mind comprehended the implication of his words. Nicholas had died, and now there was no longer a way to return the gift. She became overwhelmed with the feeling she had let her mother down.

"Did you know Nicholas?" Joe asked.

Bethany shook her head. "No, but my mother did. She had asked me to return something to him."

Joe's chin lifted with a breath of understanding. "I know it doesn't change things, but he's buried in the cemetery beside St. Paul's church if you're interested. His son, Christopher, also visits here every Christmas if he might be of any help to you. Should be here later today or tomorrow, depending on the winter storm that's headed our way."

"Thank you, Joe, but I can't stay." Bethany walked out of the store much slower this time, carrying the weight of disappointment with her. The sound from the bells offered her a slight reprieve, but the burden was still present. What was she supposed to do?

Chapter Three

Bethany studied her surroundings as she returned to her car. Projecting above the rooflines of the other buildings was a church steeple that piqued her curiosity about the cemetery. She had little time left to waste and no good reason for finding Nicholas's grave, but if seeing it gave her a sense of closure, it would be worth the extra minutes. Her heart needed confirmation that it wouldn't have made any difference when she came to Snow Valley after her mother died. Nicholas was already gone.

She turned down the road that led toward the church and pulled over in front of it. Built of light gray stone, it looked to be just large enough for a town this size. The arched front doors were painted a deep red and attached with large black hinges that gave them a formidable, yet welcoming presence. Bethany may have studied the building longer had her phone not chimed, notifying her of a new text. She looked down to see it was from Kenneth.

Did you get the gift delivered? Are you on your way home?

Bethany knew it would be faster and easier to explain the situation over the phone.

I'll call as soon as I am.
Hurry, I miss you.
I miss you, too.

Bethany smiled, then put her phone down and drove up past the doors. A tall, wrought iron fence outlined the cemetery's location alongside the church, where Joe had said it was. Through the railing, she could see the several rows of headstones the fence surrounded. She stopped her car and got out, hoping the gate wasn't locked.

Her hand raised the lever, and she gave a light push, relieved to feel no resistance as the gate swung open. Bethany didn't know where to start except at the beginning of the first row. While a cemetery wouldn't be her choice place to visit, she soon found herself mesmerized by the names of people that had gone before, the year they were born and the year they died. It was the dash in between those years that allowed her the tiniest peek into each of their lives, some whose span was much too short.

Musing that the task would be easier if the names were in alphabetical order, Bethany continued zig-zagging her way back and forth until she came to an abrupt stop. There on a headstone was the name she was looking for, Nicholas Christopher Smith. But it was the inscription underneath his name that captured her attention the most. "The Bell Maker," she read aloud, unprepared for the dizzying effects it seemed to cause. She assumed the culprit was the sudden onslaught of questions now spinning in her thoughts. *A bell maker? Like the kind on Joe's door? How did her mother know him?*

The painful reminder that she could no longer ask her mother, caused an unexpected rush of sadness to fill her eyes. Bethany found it hard to believe her mother never told her about this man with the intriguing epithet. Then again, maybe it was because she had kept herself so busy finishing school and focusing on her career, that her mother never had the chance. The future was what occupied Bethany's daily plans, not the past. Yet here she was in the middle of a cemetery among monuments that represented nothing but the past. Past dreams. Past hopes. Past lives.

It didn't take much further reflection for Bethany to realize how little she really knew about her mother's life. As her mother would have it, most of their conversations were centered solely around Bethany, never the other way around. She could only assume it was her mother's way of protecting her, always wanting her to look forward, never back, and so she did. Now, it was too late.

Bethany used the sleeve of her coat to dry the moisture that had escaped onto her cheeks. There was no question the temperatures were dropping and the wetness of her tears were making her colder. While that should have propelled her to leave more quickly, it didn't. Standing in the middle of the cemetery, her feet were stuck in a quagmire of questions and emotions, she didn't know how to rescue herself from.

"Are you all right, Miss?"

Bethany's head whipped around toward the voice that jolted her from her thoughts. An older gentleman with a gray beard, wearing a dark wool overcoat and a flat tweed cap was standing outside the side entrance to the church.

She nodded, trying to convince herself as much as him.

"Not too many people visit the cemetery this time of year," he said, slowly approaching her.

It was then that Bethany noticed the white clerical collar, identifying him as a priest.

"They call me Father Alan," he said, extending his arm forward.

She took his hand and shook it. "My name is Bethany."

"I don't believe I've seen you here before, have I?" he asked.

"No, this is my first time in Snow Valley. I was just on my way out of town, but it was nice to meet you Father Alan," she answered, starting to step away from the grave.

"If you were here to pay your respects to Nicholas, they couldn't have gone to a better man," Father Alan said. "He and his wife, Amelie, never met a stranger, willing to open their home to anyone that needed a place to stay."

His words caused Bethany to stop and look back at Nicholas's headstone before shifting her eyes to the one next to it. Amelie Marie Smith, she read, then studied the dates. "I see Amelie died quite a few years before Nicholas."

Father Alan nodded. "That she did, but just like Nicholas and his ancestors before him, she'll never be forgotten. They are how this town got its nickname."

The corner of Bethany's mouth lifted into a knowing smile, remembering Joe's teasing when she first entered his store. "Let me guess. Smithville?"

"You're a good guesser," Father Alan chuckled, accentuating the soft creases around his eyes. "May I offer you a cup of coffee or hot chocolate to warm you up before you go?"

"Oh no, but thank you anyway. I have to get back to the city," she declined, though it did sound nice. She hadn't had anything to eat or drink since the quick bowl of cereal she grabbed for breakfast.

"I can offer you a blueberry muffin, too. Our secretary, Mrs. Snyder, bakes the best there are," he said with increasing persuasion.

Bethany felt her resolve weakening. It was as if he knew she had an empty space inside her that needed filling, besides her stomach. "Okay, coffee and a muffin it is, as long as it doesn't take too long."

Father Alan grinned. "Trust me, you won't be sorry."

Bethany checked the time as they walked toward the church, convincing herself a few more minutes in Snow Valley couldn't hurt. The door they entered placed them in a hallway from which she could see two offices. She was right behind Father Alan when he turned into the first one.

"Mrs. Snyder, we have a guest I would like you to meet. This is Bethany."

Mrs. Snyder stood up and came around her desk, wearing large round glasses and a warm smile. "It's nice to meet you Bethany. What brings you to Snow Valley?"

She hesitated, unsure how to answer, and was grateful when Father Alan spoke up for her. "Nicholas Smith, yes?" He looked at Bethany to confirm.

"Yes," she answered.

"Such a lovely, sweet man, he was. Anyone would count themselves lucky to have known him." Mrs. Snyder's voice was teeming with affection.

While it was true Nicholas was the reason she was there, Bethany didn't want either of them thinking it was her who had known him. "Actually, it was my mother who knew him," she clarified.

"Then lucky for her." Mrs. Snyder responded with another smile. "I just made a fresh pot of coffee, and there are blueberry muffins for the taking, at least for one of you."

Father Alan winked at Bethany. "Mrs. Snyder has taken it upon herself to watch out for my well-being."

"Somebody has to do it," Mrs. Snyder laughed.

"I must admit she's given me ample opportunities to practice resisting temptation, which can only be good for my soul and my waistline," Father Alan added with his own laughter. "So how about that coffee and muffin for one?"

Chapter Four

Father Alan led Bethany into his office where she took a seat close to his desk to enjoy the coffee and blueberry muffin, Mrs. Snyder promptly brought in. He hadn't been exaggerating when he said the muffins were the best there were. Loaded with delicious wild blueberries and topped with sweet buttery crumbs made them the picture and taste of perfection.

"You mentioned your mother knowing Nicholas. Did she live in Snow Valley at one time?" Father Alan's voice rose with the question.

Bethany's mind struggled to form an answer while she swallowed another bite. "I don't really know. If she did, it would have been a long time ago."

Father Alan rested back in his chair. "Not many people come to Snow Valley by accident, but we welcome all who do, no matter the reason."

"Thank you," she said, gleaning that his words were meant for both her mother and her.

Bethany finished another sip of coffee, taking a longer look at this man whose kindness was more genuine than any she could remember. The world she worked and lived in, was filled with stipulations, usually self-serving ones. She had just met Father Alan, yet she had the distinct impression she could trust him regarding anything, not only his opinion on blueberry muffins.

While she was eager to get back to Kenneth and their beach vacation, Bethany was equally as eager to see her promise through as best she could. Even though returning the gift to Nicholas was no longer possible, it didn't feel right to do nothing. A growing awareness that the gift didn't belong to her and never would, challenged her further.

Her eyes fell to her purse where she could see the corners of gold wrapping peeking through. Unable to withstand the dilemma any longer, Bethany reached for the box when a knock on the door suddenly stopped her.

"I hope I'm not interrupting, but the latest weather forecast says the storm is coming in much earlier than they anticipated," Mrs. Snyder informed them.

Bethany glanced between Mrs. Snyder's and Father Alan's concerned expressions and popped up from her chair. Dilemma or not, she had no choice but to leave. "I better hurry then. Thank you again for everything."

Mrs. Snyder was quick on her heels. "But hon, you shouldn't be driving through the mountains now. These storms are hard to predict and can be dangerous when they first blow in. Why don't you rest up here for the night, and see how the roads are in the morning? They'll start plowing pretty early, especially with ski season upon us.

"I wish I could, but my boyfriend and I have plans with his family, and then a plane to catch," Bethany said.

Father Alan walked over to join them. "The radar shows it hitting this entire area. Are you sure we can't talk you into staying?"

"I'll be fine. I've driven in snow plenty of times," she reassured them.

Mrs. Snyder peered over her glasses. "I don't like the sound of you being on the highway alone, but at least let me wrap up another muffin for you to take."

Bethany smiled. "Those, you would never have to talk me into." She watched Mrs. Snyder step out of the office and turned her attention to Father Alan, "I do want to come back to Snow Valley…maybe after the snow season."

Father Alan smiled. "We would love that. And if there's more to the story that brought you here, I hope you'll share it next time."

She nodded as Mrs. Snyder returned with a small sack and a piece of paper. "Here you go, a muffin and a phone number in case you run into trouble. It rings at the church and at the rectory. You be careful now."

"I will." Bethany's gaze held hers for a moment longer until she left the office and was out the door that led back through the cemetery. Her eyes passed over the rows, pausing where Nicholas was buried. "I wish I could have met you. I'm truly sorry about the gift," she whispered to herself.

Bethany's eyes moved upward to witness the sky growing heavier with clouds. At least she would be driving out of the mountains and not into them. She quickly got into her car and pulled out her phone to call Kenneth.

"I was about to file a missing person's report," he answered.

"Sorry, the trip turned out to be more complicated than I expected," Bethany explained, starting the engine.

"At least you got the promise to your mother taken care of and you never have to go back to Snow Valley again," Kenneth said.

Bethany hesitated, preparing herself for his response. "About that promise…I didn't get to deliver the gift after all."

Kenneth released his frustration into the phone. "I knew it would turn out to be a waste of time. There's no telling how your mother's medications were affecting her mind."

"That's not it," she replied, uncomfortable with the insinuation her mother was delusional. "The man I was to deliver the gift to passed away a few years ago. At least I got to visit his grave."

"You went to a cemetery? You really do need a vacation," he chided.

That was all the response Bethany needed to hear to decide against telling Kenneth about the unusual inscription on Nicholas's headstone. He would likely only make fun of that as well. "I better be hurrying since there's a storm on its way. I'll call again when I've reached the city."

"Hey, I am sorry things didn't work out for you," Kenneth said in a more contrite manner.

"Me, too. See you soon." Bethany hung up and drove away from the church, slowing down as she passed Joe's Country Store. A strange and conflicting feeling swept over her as she did, one that seemed to be warning her she was leaving too late and too soon at the same time.

She did her best to dismiss the feeling by trying to find a radio station within range. Bethany wanted to get updates on the weather, but more than that, she wanted to listen to Christmas music. After several attempts, she gave up and made her own music, beginning with "Angels We Have Heard on High," singing out especially loud on the chorus.

The songs kept her mind occupied while attempting to ignore the snowflakes that began to fall against the windshield. It was true she had driven in the snow many times, though never in the mountains. She reduced her speed as a precaution, but the noticeable absence of other cars was almost eerie.

Pretty soon not even "Jingle Bells" could allay Bethany's nerves. The car's wipers were no longer able to keep up with the growing accumulation of snow, making it difficult to see the road in front of her. It wasn't until Bethany was right upon the set of flashing lights that she realized she had come to a barricade. The road had been closed and for good reason. All she could see ahead of her was the color white.

Bethany was officially frightened, now understanding how easily one could get lost, or worse, in a blizzard. She couldn't say Father Alan and Mrs. Snyder hadn't advised against her leaving. For all her confidence, Bethany realized it would never be a match against the forces of nature. There was nothing she could do but turn her car around and try heading back toward Snow Valley.

Thankfully, the snow didn't seem as blinding, driving in the opposite direction. Bethany picked up the piece of paper Mrs. Snyder had handed her and decided to tell her she was on her way back. At least if she never showed up, they would know to come looking for her. The small blanket she kept in her car along with the extra muffin would help her survive for a while.

Bethany dialed the number. "Mrs. Snyder. This is—"

"Bethany, I'm so relieved to hear from you. We got word about the road closing not long after you left. Are you all right? Where are you?" her words poured out at once.

"I'm okay. I just turned around at the barricade," she answered.

"Listen, you take it slow and easy. I've notified Joe and he's already on his way. Keep an eye out for a white plow truck, and he'll have you safely back here in no time," Mrs. Snyder instructed.

Bethany was overcome with gratitude that someone who barely knew her would care so much about her safety. Suddenly, she didn't feel as alone anymore and couldn't help but chuckle. "Would that be Joe or Joe Jr.?"

Mrs. Snyder responded with her own light chuckle. "I see you've already met those two ornery fellows. That would be plain old Joe," she answered. "Don't you worry, he's been plowing these roads for decades."

"Thank you, Mrs. Snyder." Bethany loosened the knuckled grip she had on her steering wheel and tried to relax, knowing help was on its way. She only had one thing left to worry about, Kenneth.

Chapter Five

Keeping an eye out for a white truck in a world quickly transforming to all white was close to impossible. The tracks her car may have left on the road had long been filled in. Bethany looked to the trees on either side of her that weren't completely covered in snow to help her maintain her bearings. As long as she kept moving and singing, she was able to convince herself she would be okay. Knowing Joe was somewhere up ahead, clearing the road, was also an enormous comfort.

Bethany thought back to earlier in the fall when she received her first big promotion and decided to purchase a new car. Kenneth had gone with her to pick it out and scoffed at the idea that she wanted to buy one that was four-wheeled drive, since his vehicle was already equipped that way. He tried to talk her into a much sleeker looking sedan instead, both less useful and more expensive. This was one time she was glad she hadn't listened to him.

It didn't seem much longer before Bethany noticed an orange flag waving in the air and coming towards her. The closer it got, the better she could see the outline of a white plow truck with the flag flying above its roof. It had to be

Joe. He slowed to a stop and rolled down his window. Bethany stopped beside him and grinned at how different he looked, wearing a fur-lined trapper hat on his head.

"I'm mighty glad to see you're all right," he said.

"Thank you for coming to help me, Joe. I don't know what I would have done..." Bethany's voice trailed off.

"Don't give it another thought. If I hadn't found you, my wife along with the rest of Snow Valley would have joined the search until we did," he assured her. "Now, let's hurry and get you in front of the warm fire I know she has waiting for you. I'm going to turn around, and then you follow right behind me."

Bethany watched as Joe maneuvered his truck in front of her and began leading her back to town. Feeling tethered to this man and his plow truck, soon dispelled any remaining fear. She had never known the kind of peace inherent in complete trust, yet she was experiencing it from people, that until today, she didn't know existed.

It wasn't long before she found herself humming the tune of "Let it Snow" and laughed. There was no question the weather was frightful, but Bethany was no longer scared of freezing to death and was looking forward to the warm fire Joe said was waiting for her. A few hours earlier, the thought of being stuck in Snow Valley for the night would have filled her with nothing but disappointment. Something had changed, however, and she found herself looking forward to it instead.

While Bethany was still excited to spend Christmas in the Caribbean with Kenneth, if she were being truthful, she didn't mind missing the time they were to spend with his parents beforehand. While they had always been nice enough, that was the problem. They treated her the same way they would anyone, nothing like how Bethany expected a potential new member of the family would be treated. Maybe once she was wearing an engagement ring on her finger, they would act differently toward her.

As they entered the town, Bethany continued following Joe past the church and his country store to the intersection where he then turned left. Her eyes shifted from one side of the street to the other until Joe pulled next to the curb in front of a pale, yellow house and stopped. He got out of his truck and motioned for her to park in its driveway. Bethany assumed the house must be Joe's, with the smoke billowing from the chimney, indicating the fire inside. She was sure Joe's wife would be as kind as he had been.

Bethany felt stiff, opening the car's door and standing up. She hadn't realized how tense she must have been, not only from driving into a blizzard, but from everything else she had learned that day. Above all, finding out Nicholas had passed away, and she wouldn't be able to return the gift to him.

"My wife is a strong woman of purpose, but don't let that overwhelm you. She has the biggest heart of anyone I've known and will be awfully glad to see you safe and sound," Joe said right before he opened the front door.

The warmth drew Bethany inside where she was immediately greeted.

"Oh, you poor dear," the woman said, taking quick hold of Bethany's hands.

"Mrs. Snyder!" she exclaimed, needing a moment to recognize her without her glasses on. Bethany then looked at Joe. "For some reason I thought you were taking me to your house."

Joe gave her a sheepish grin. "This is my house."

"Joe Snyder, did you not tell Bethany I would be here?" Mrs. Snyder's head tilted in mock consternation as she asked the question.

"I thought she knew you were my wife," he answered, innocently.

Bethany shook her head, then burst out laughing. "So, you and Mrs. Snyder are married."

"Best forty years of my life," Joe confirmed with a gleam in his eyes.

"And he's called me Mrs. Snyder every day during those forty years. Said he liked the sound of it so much, he never wanted to stop saying it," she added, her eyes gleaming back at his.

Joe seemed to blush, though the reddish hues still present from the cold provided him some cover. "You can't blame me now. I never thought you'd say yes."

"And I thought you'd never ask," Mrs. Snyder responded with a wink, then returned her attention to Bethany. "Come and sit next to the fire while I whip up something to eat. You must be starving by now."

"Not too badly, since you gave me another muffin to eat," Bethany said, smiling, "but I should probably call Kenneth first to let him know where I am and that I'll be spending the night in Snow Valley."

"Of course, let me show you the bedroom you'll be staying in, where you can call and have some privacy. It's right down this hallway." Mrs. Snyder was already heading that direction.

Bethany followed behind her into a room with cream colored walls, and a colorful patchwork quilt spread across a four-poster bed. A nightstand and a small table and chair completed the furnishings. Breathing in the vision, she couldn't have felt more welcome.

"I love this room. Did it used to belong to one of your children?" Bethany asked.

"No, dear." Her voice was quieter. "Joe and I don't have any children."

Bethany was embarrassed she might have said something upsetting to Mrs. Snyder. "I'm sorry, I never should have presumed you did."

"Oh honey, there's no need to apologize," she assured her with a wave of her hand. "We may not have been able to raise our own children, but there's been plenty of guests and others around here that have needed looking after."

Bethany's eyebrows rose with the corners of her mouth. "Does that include Father Alan?"

Mrs. Snyder leaned her head back with a laugh. "*Especially* Father Alan, but only where his eating habits are concerned. Bless him, he does like his sweets. I will leave you to your phone call now, I do hope you'll feel at home while you're here."

"Mrs. Snyder," Bethany called out, stopping her at the doorway. "I can't think of a place I'd rather be."

Chapter Six

Bethany's smile fell as soon as Mrs. Snyder left the room. She dreaded having to tell Kenneth there would be no dinner with his parents tonight. Despite knowing the snowstorm and the road closing weren't her fault, she did feel responsible for waiting too long to come to Snow Valley and then waiting too long to leave.

The sooner she called, the sooner she could return to the fire and Joe and Mrs. Snyder's company. Bethany took her phone from her purse and pressed his number. It hadn't rung more than once before she heard Kenneth's voice.

"Please tell me you're almost here."

Bethany cringed at his words. "I wish I could."

"How far out are you? The snow is starting to come down pretty heavy now. If we don't leave for my parents' soon, we'll have to wait until tomorrow."

Her eyes closed then opened with her next breath, creating a long pause.

"Bethany, are you still there?"

"Yes, I'm here. We're going to have to wait until tomorrow anyway, Kenneth. I'm still in Snow Valley."

"But you were on your way back when I last talked to you."

"I was, but the storm moved in faster and stronger than was predicted, and they closed the road. I didn't have a choice but to turn around and come back." When he didn't respond right away, she continued. "Hopefully, the roads will get plowed early enough in the morning that we'll still have plenty of time with your parents before we have to fly out."

"I guess that will have to work, besides that I could use more time to finish my report."

"Okay, I'll call in the morning. I miss you."

"Miss you, too."

Bethany hung up and gave herself a minute before she returned to the living room. She was thankful Kenneth hadn't sounded too upset, but there was something in their conversation, that bothered her. Or more what *wasn't* in it. He didn't even ask where she was staying or express any concern about her safety. Then again maybe she was being too hard on him. He probably assumed she was in a motel and didn't know how dangerous the storms could be in the mountains. She sure didn't.

Joe was putting another log on the fire when she walked back into the living room. She heard it hiss and pop as it came to life, at the same time she smelled a mouthwatering aroma coming from the kitchen. Through the dining room, she could see Mrs. Snyder standing at the stove, stirring something.

"Whatever it is you're making, it smells delicious. If I wasn't starving before, I am now," Bethany said, joining her.

Mrs. Snyder turned from browning the ground beef to look at her and smile. "It's called Blizzard Stew, the easiest thing in the world to make and perfect for this kind of weather."

"May I help?" Bethany asked.

"If you'd like to open those cans of soup, we'll add them to the Dutch oven with the rest of the ingredients and let the whole thing simmer a bit." Mrs. Snyder said, pointing to a can opener on top of the counter.

Bethany proceeded to open, then empty each one over the seasoned beef and start stirring.

"I see Mrs. Snyder put you to work," Joe observed from the doorway.

"This is hardly what I'd call work. I'd be happy to do so much more," Bethany said with a generous dose of enthusiasm.

Mrs. Snyder laughed. "Be careful what you offer or Joe will have you taking inventory and stocking shelves at the store."

Bethany laughed as well. "If I was going to be here longer, I would insist. That would be the least I could do to thank you for taking in a complete stranger."

"No one is a stranger here," Joe responded with a grin before going back to the living room.

Mrs. Snyder took bowls and plates from the cabinet and set placemats and silverware on the table. "It looks like we're ready to eat as soon as I slice and butter some homemade bread."

Bethany began ladling the stew into the bowls, helping to carry them into the dining room. She was glad her chair put her in full view of the fireplace while she ate. Neither her apartment nor Kenneth's home had one.

After a few bites, she spoke up. "You're right Mrs. Snyder, this is the perfect meal for a snowy day."

"One that doesn't look to be ending any time soon, I'm afraid," Joe said with his eyes turned toward the window.

Bethany looked for herself. Though it had grown dark, one could easily see the snow illuminated by the streetlight, falling just as hard, if not harder than it was earlier.

"Now Joe, don't be causing any extra worry for Bethany and Kenneth. Only the good Lord knows what tomorrow will bring."

"Right as always, Mrs. Snyder," Joe said with a wink.

They continued eating until everyone had finished. "Can I get you more stew, Bethany?" Mrs. Snyder asked as she started to clear the table.

"As tempting as that is, my stomach is happily full," she answered, "though I will have to write down the recipe, as well as the one for the blueberry muffins, if it isn't a secret."

Mrs. Snyder shook her head. "I don't believe recipes should ever be kept a secret. I would love to share the muffin recipe with you. It would be like wishing on the same star, knowing we may be mixing up a batch at the same time, no matter where we find ourselves. In the meantime, why don't you go enjoy the fire while I clean up."

"But I—"

"No buts this time, it will take me just a few minutes."

Joe smiled and pointed his thumb toward the fireplace. "You may as well surrender."

Bethany laughed and chose the chair closest to the fire, which happened to be a rocking chair. She couldn't remember the last time she had sat in one and instinctively began the back and forth motion while Joe walked over to the stereo on the other side of the room.

"Hope you don't mind a little Christmas music. Mrs. Snyder and I can't seem to get enough of it this time of year."

"Me, too, it's my favorite." Bethany said, watching him pull an album from its sleeve and place it on the record player. She didn't know if she had ever felt this level of coziness before. She only knew she would never have felt this way at Kenneth's parents' house.

Bethany didn't realize the effect the rocking would have until her eyes opened sometime later. Joe and Mrs. Snyder were both reading books from the sofa across from her and a crocheted blanket had been laid across her lap.

"I'm glad you got some rest. Driving in the snow can be stressful," Mrs. Snyder said.

Bethany sat up to further shake herself awake. "How long did I sleep?"

"Both sides of Bing Crosby and one of Andy Williams, so I reckon at least an hour," Joe answered as a gust of wind whistled through the screens on the windows.

Remembering Mrs. Snyder's comment on what tomorrow might bring, Bethany resisted saying anything about the weather. Instead, she turned her thoughts to the reason she ended up in this situation in the first place. If she couldn't give the gift to Nicholas, maybe having to stay the night was her chance to do the next right thing.

"You mentioned Nicholas Smith had a son named Christopher that visits this time of year. Do you think there's a chance I could meet him if he's in town before I leave?"

Joe voiced a soft grunt. "I heard he actually made it in today, just ahead of the storm. I imagine he'll be in the store tomorrow to get some supplies. I could put in a good word for you."

Bethany smiled then nodded. "I would like that. After all the nice things I've heard about Nicholas, I assume Christopher must be the same way."

Joe looked at his wife, prompting Bethany to do the same. Mrs. Snyder's wary expression was accompanied by a deep breath.

"Did I say something wrong?" Bethany asked, her eyes looking to each of them for an answer.

"Not at all," Joe answered with a shake of his head. "Unfortunately, Christopher isn't much like his father. He's more of a crusty sort that prefers to keep to himself while he's here."

"Let's just say he's one of those needing looked after, even if he doesn't think so," Mrs. Snyder added.

Bethany's mind sifted through what she had been told. She couldn't imagine what would make Christopher so different than his father "That's okay, Joe, I'm not afraid of crusty. All I know is if there is any chance to meet him, I have to try."

"Then we'll do our best," Joe said, standing from the sofa. "I think I better call it a night, seeing as how early I'm going to have to start plowing. See you in the morning."

"Good night." Bethany watched him walk through the kitchen to what must be another bedroom. As reluctant as she was to leave the comfort of the fireplace and the rocking chair, she knew she should be going to bed as well. "I suppose I should get plenty of sleep for tomorrow, too."

Mrs. Snyder smiled. "It's a good idea for all of us. There are fresh towels in the bathroom, and flannel pajamas on top of your bed to sleep in if you'd like."

Bethany stood and folded the blanket over the chair. "You're a life saver, Mrs. Snyder. Even if I hadn't left my suitcase with Kenneth, all I had packed were beach clothes to take to the Caribbean. I don't think they would have come in very handy right now."

Mrs. Snyder chuckled. "If you need anything else at all, you just ask."

Bethany nodded, then left for her bedroom. She was relieved not to have to sleep in her clothes. It was bad enough she would have to be wearing them again the next day.

She found the pair of red plaid pajamas folded neatly at the end of the bed and took them into the bathroom to change. Bethany smiled when she saw a toothbrush and toothpaste sitting on top of the towel and washcloth, as well as a bar of soap. It was obvious Mrs. Snyder was always prepared to take care of guests, planned or unplanned.

Bethany returned to the room and hung her clothes in the closet before turning off the lamp. She was surprised how light the room still was and walked over to the window. The snow showed no signs of slowing down much less stopping. While Bethany didn't want to worry, the same question persisted in her thoughts.

Just what *was* tomorrow going to bring?

Chapter Seven

Bethany reached for her phone to check the time. It was only 7:00 a.m., but she was wide awake and could hear the soft, sputtering sounds of coffee brewing in the kitchen. Knowing she needed an early start to the day, Bethany threw back the bedcovers and grabbed the robe she had seen in the closet.

Going to the window first, she pushed the curtains aside and sucked in her next breath. Everything had been blanketed by inches, if not feet, of the icy, white crystals. Bethany stood and stared a moment longer, awed and alarmed at the same time. At least it was no longer snowing, and she could see where Joe had already plowed the street in front of the house. She hoped that meant all the other roads had been plowed as well.

The aroma of coffee finally pulled Bethany away from the window and toward the kitchen where she saw Mrs. Snyder sitting at the small table. "Good morning."

Mrs. Snyder looked at her and smiled. "Good morning, I'm glad you found the robe. Did you sleep well?"

Bethany nodded. "I guess I was more tired than I realized."

"Let me pour you a cup of coffee," Mrs. Snyder said, starting to stand.

Bethany gently placed her hand on Mrs. Snyder's shoulder to stop her. "I can get it and refill yours while I'm at it."

She picked up the almost empty cup in front of Mrs. Snyder and continued over to the coffee maker, surprised to see it wasn't the usual drip kind. It was a percolator, similar to one she remembered her mother once having. Once Bethany stirred cream and sugar into her cup, she added more black coffee to the other and placed them on the table as she sat down.

"How early did Joe start plowing this morning?" Bethany asked.

Mrs. Snyder's eyebrows rose. "He was in his truck by 4:00 a.m."

"That's early all right," she laughed. "How much longer do you think it will take to plow the main roads?"

"Bethany..." Mrs. Snyder began, then paused as if carefully measuring her next words. "Last night, we had a record breaking—"

The front door suddenly opened, interrupting any further conversation. They both looked through the kitchen doorway to see Joe heading toward them.

"I'm not sure Snow Valley hasn't been confused with the North Pole," he said, blowing on his hands and rubbing them together before he continued, "I'm sorry for the bad news."

Mrs. Snyder's head tipped to the side. "I hadn't quite finished telling her, Joe."

Bethany's eyes widened as she searched their faces for answers. "What bad news?"

Joe hung his head before raising it again to explain. "There's too much snow to plow for the roads to open today. Even with some extra trucks, it's taking twice as long to clear them than usual. I'm sorry, Bethany, I know how much you wanted to get home."

Bethany couldn't believe what she was hearing. "Is there any other way back to the city? I don't care how long it takes."

"If there is, you can be sure Joe will find it and have you on your way," Mrs. Snyder answered.

Despite Mrs. Snyder's consoling confidence, it took a long, deep breath for Bethany to reign in another round of dread. Kenneth was likely going to be much less understanding this time when she told him the news.

"Kenneth booked our flight for late tomorrow afternoon, so as long as I drive straight to the airport when the roads open, there should still be plenty of time for us to catch it." Bethany was trying to think positive until she noticed that Joe's and Mrs. Snyder's distressed expressions hadn't changed. She felt her heart sink again. "I get the feeling there is more bad news you haven't finished giving me."

"Mind you the forecast has been wrong many times," Mrs. Snyder spoke up first, "but, the radar is showing another wave of snow on its way. It's predicted to drop just as much as it did last night."

Bethany could tell how difficult it was for them to tell her, even though it certainly wasn't their fault she may have to stay longer. She raised her chin and managed a smile.

"Then I intend to make the most of my time here, helping out while learning all about Snow Valley. The busier I can be, the better."

"But you are our guest." Mrs. Snyder returned a relieved smile.

"Not today." Bethany stood up from the table. "In fact, I'm going to go ahead and get dressed, so I'll be ready."

"Bethany, hon..." Mrs. Snyder called out.

Bethany had already started to leave the kitchen when she turned back around.

Mrs. Snyder's eyes twinkled as she peered above her glasses. "I think you're going to need some suitable clothes to wear if you plan on being out in all this snow."

Bethany's hand flew to her mouth, causing them all to break into laughter. "I forgot I don't have any."

"Don't you worry, I've got extra socks and snow boots you can borrow as well as some flannel-lined pants and a sweater. If those don't work, we can check the clothes closet at the church," Mrs. Snyder offered.

Bethany's curiosity was suddenly piqued. "You have a clothes closet at the church?"

Mrs. Snyder seemed a touch embarrassed. "It's really just a small room in the basement, but we like to call it our closet. It's where we keep our donated clothes and shoes for anyone who finds themselves needing to borrow some. I'll go gather what I have while Joe starts the bacon. It isn't the kind of day any of us should start on an empty stomach."

Bethany sat back down at the table to watch Joe pull bacon from the refrigerator and lay the strips inside a skillet. "How much plowing were you able to do so far?"

"Mostly just the main streets, but enough for most people to get around if they have to," he answered as the bacon began to sizzle. "I'll be opening up the store just as soon as we eat breakfast."

"Don't be surprised if I show up there a little later to try and catch Christopher Smith myself."

Before Joe could respond, Mrs. Snyder came bustling back into the kitchen carrying a stack of clothes and a pair of boots in her arms. "I'm sure none of these would have ever made the cover of a fashion magazine, but they're practical and will keep you warm and dry if nothing else. Why don't you give them a try while I get the eggs and toast ready?"

"Thank you." Bethany took the armful of items and went to her room, knowing it wouldn't matter how many more times she said those words, it was never going to feel like enough.

She jumped when her phone started ringing, not expecting Kenneth to be awake, yet there was his name glaring at her. Her thumb hovered above the screen a few seconds until she finally pressed the button.

"You're up bright and early this morning," she answered.

"I just can't wait for you to get here," he laughed. "When are you leaving?"

Bethany closed her eyes to speak again. "It looks like I may have to meet you at the airport tomorrow."

"What are you talking about? Why aren't you coming today?"

"There's too much snow to plow in order for the roads to reopen. If there was another way, I would take it. I hope you can understand."

"I'm trying to Bethany, but none of this would have happened if you hadn't gone to Snow Valley in the first place. I know you were trying to return something for your mother, but was it really worth risking our plans? I mean have you even found out what was in the box yet?" Kenneth questioned her with a sharp edge of impatience in his voice.

"No, but I found out the man I was supposed to give it to has a son in town, and I'm hoping to give it to him. At least whatever it is will be staying in the family." Bethany knew her defense was weak.

"That's great, Bethany. Listen, I'll talk to you later, after I've explained to my mother why you aren't going to be here…again."

Bethany didn't need to hang up, Kenneth already had for her. She didn't know how to make him understand why this trip was so important. But then again, she would have to understand why, herself.

Chapter Eight

Tears threatened to form, but Bethany willed them back by looking at the stack of clothes Mrs. Snyder had given her to wear. The kindness she had discovered in Snow Valley was one she was determined to hold onto, no matter how unhappy Kenneth might be or what the future brought.

Bethany started trying on the clothes as her conversation with Kenneth repeated itself in her mind. They had never had a disagreement like this before that she could recall. Whether that was good or bad, she wasn't sure, but Bethany knew most relationships were tested at one time or another. By the time she slipped the sweater over her head, Bethany had decided if they could survive this one, they could survive any other tests that came their way.

She sat on the edge of the bed to put the socks and boots on, then stood up to take a look at herself in the mirror. The clothes were a little big, but they fit well enough. Most important, they were warm.

Bethany entered the kitchen and lifted her nose to the smell of buttered toast, mingling with the bacon and eggs. "I'm ready for the snow now, and for breakfast."

"I'm so glad to see the clothes worked out all right." Mrs. Snyder said while setting out the plates and silverware. "Come sit down while I put everything on the table."

Joe sat down in the chair beside Bethany. "What do you ladies plan to do today?"

"I thought we would first go by the church, to make sure the garlands and wreaths are on schedule for the hanging of the greens, along with checking on the poinsettia delivery," Mrs. Snyder answered before looking at Bethany. "You should see how beautifully the church is decorated for the Christmas Eve service."

The words *Christmas Eve* caused a lump to form in Bethany's throat. Resisting the flood of mixed emotions, she turned her head to peer back into the living area. "Will you be putting up a Christmas tree?"

"We try not to hurry Christmas here like a lot of other places, but I do believe it's time, don't you agree, Mrs. Snyder?" Joe asked, between a forkful of his eggs and bacon.

"I think tonight would be perfect. That way Bethany could help us." Mrs. Snyder's attention shifted to Bethany. "That is if you would like to."

Bethany couldn't swallow her bite of toast fast enough. "I would love to help. Do we need to put it together first?"

Joe released a hearty chuckle. "Oh, nature does a pretty good job of that already. I'll have one delivered from the lot this afternoon."

"A real one?" Bethany looked at Mrs. Snyder, unable to contain the anticipation. "Can we pick it out?"

Mrs. Snyder's eyes seemed to glisten with her response. "Of course, we can. I have a coat to get you by this morning, but while we're at the church, we should check the clothes closet for one that might fit you better."

"And I should be heading to the store to make sure the shelves are stocked and ready for customers." Joe stood up from the table, lifting his hand in a quick wave. "I will see you two, later."

Bethany hadn't forgotten how much she hoped one of those customers would be Christopher. She gathered the empty plates and carried them to the sink to be rinsed off. "I'll go finish getting ready for the day. It sounds like we have lots to do."

She left the kitchen to go to the bedroom, thankful she always carried an extra hairbrush in her purse, along with a ponytail holder to pull back her long and naturally wavy hair. Bethany unzipped the purse's opening and felt an unexpected tingling of goosebumps when her eyes fell on the wrapped gift first. She lifted the box out and held it for a moment before setting it aside. Somehow, she would make sure Christopher received it.

After fixing her hair, Bethany returned the gift to her purse and brought it with her into the living room where Mrs. Snyder was waiting for her with a jacket, and all the accessories she could need, including gloves, a scarf and a hat. "I didn't want to take the chance of you getting cold. Do you mind walking to the church?"

"I would love that. The snow never stays pretty for very long in the city," Bethany said already zipping up the jacket. Once she had put the rest of the items on, she picked her purse back up, ready to go.

"You could leave that here if you'd like," Mrs. Snyder suggested.

Bethany grinned. "You never know, I might want to make a purchase at this place called Joe's Country store."

Mrs. Snyder laughed. "You just might."

They stepped out the front door and giggled when their feet sank in the snow up to their knees. There were children already outside, building snowmen and forts for snowball fights in front of their homes. As Bethany watched and listened to their playful chatter, it made her wonder if she had ever built either one when she was younger. Sadly, she couldn't remember.

It was only a few blocks to the church, and they were soon on main street, heading that direction. Bethany took note of the shops they passed by along the way, hoping to someday stop inside a few of them. As soon as they were beyond Joe's store, they turned up the hill and went to the same entrance Bethany had come through the day before.

Mrs. Snyder unlocked the door, but instead of continuing toward the offices, it was down a stairway to another door where Bethany followed her.

"Mind you it's a bit of a mess in here. Maybe after the holidays, I'll have a chance to get it organized," she said before opening the door.

Bethany had no idea what to expect, but was surprised to enter a room about the size of a small bedroom with shoes of all kinds, lined up or in boxes against the wall, and several racks of hanging clothes. She went to one of the racks and brushed her hand across the fabrics, certain each item had a story to tell.

She lifted one of the hangers to take a closer look at a long, double-breasted coat made of camel-colored wool. It was still in great condition. "How old are these?"

"I'm sure some of them are as old as I am," Mrs. Snyder answered with a reminiscent look.

Bethany continued to pick through the racks, surveying all the varieties and styles. "You could open up a vintage clothing store with these." But no sooner had Bethany's words left her mouth that she realized the insinuation. "I mean not that you are vintage or anything."

Mrs. Snyder burst into full blown laughter. "Oh honey, I'm vintage all right, but hopefully, like a fine wine, I've gotten better with age."

Bethany smiled as an idea popped into her thoughts. "I bet you could sell some of these if you wanted to."

"I'm afraid they've become too much like old friends for that. Some of them have been borrowed and returned more times than I can count," Mrs. Snyder responded a bit wistfully.

"I was just thinking the money could be used to expand the closet, if you wanted to," Bethany said.

Mrs. Snyder's forehead drew together at the suggestion. "Do you really think there are people who would buy old used clothing?"

"You would be surprised." Bethany's eyes returned to the wool coat she had been drawn to earlier. She picked the hanger up again. "Would you mind if I tried this one on?"

"Of course not. It's definitely been a favorite through the years. Someday, I'll have to look back through the registry and count how many times it's been borrowed. It's such a nice coat that I'm always a little surprised when it shows back up."

"So, you keep records of all the clothes?" Bethany asked while she slipped her arms inside the sleeves and began to secure the buttons down the front.

Mrs. Snyder nodded, thoughtfully. "I have since the church first opened the closet, but it hasn't been as much for the clothes, as it has been for the people who borrowed them. Anyone who visits the closet has some kind of need, even if it's just because they've gotten stranded here in a snowstorm." She paused to grin at Bethany. "We like to remember them all by name as if they've become part of our family."

Bethany displayed her own grin at having finished buttoning the coat's last button. She then spread her arms out and turned around. "I think it fits."

A brief moment of bewilderment seemed to pass between them before Mrs. Snyder crossed her arms and leaned her head to the side. "I'd say it more than just fits. If I didn't know better, I'd say it was made especially for you. Never mind that it would have been before you were born, maybe even before your mother was."

They both laughed, though the innocent mention of her mother tempered its sweetness for Bethany. Mrs. Snyder wouldn't know her mother had recently passed away, or that her words were a sober reminder of her unfulfilled mission.

"I thought I heard some familiar voices of laughter coming from inside here," a voice spoke from the doorway into the room.

Bethany's entire body whipped around. "Hi, Father Alan."

"I hear you get to stay in Snow Valley another night. We might make a permanent resident out of you yet," he remarked.

"I'm afraid that's only wishful thinking, Father. Remember, this young woman has both a boyfriend and a job in the city," Mrs. Snyder reminded him.

Bethany smiled. "That won't stop me from visiting again, and while I'm here, I've decided to help organize all these clothes."

Father Alan returned Bethany's smile. "I better let you two go to work then. I'll be in my office if either of you need anything."

His words caused Bethany to glance at her purse. She did need something, just as soon as she finished the closet.

Chapter Nine

"You don't need to do any work, Bethany. I'll have plenty of time after the first of the year to organize this room." Mrs. Snyder tried to convince her otherwise.

"I think it will be fun," Bethany countered, her enthusiasm contagious. "Besides being a good way to get my mind off of Kenneth."

Mrs. Snyder's mouth formed an expression, hovering between reluctance and surrender. "All right, but as soon as I check on the greenery, I'll be right back to help you."

Bethany smiled. "Don't worry, I'll be fine."

Mrs. Snyder didn't move right away, seeming hesitant to leave.

"Remember, we still have a Christmas tree to pick out today," Bethany encouraged her.

"You're right," Mrs. Snyder said with a renewed sense of purpose. "Feel free to organize things however you think is best. I'm just thankful you found a nice coat to borrow."

With that, Mrs. Snyder finally walked out of the room, giving Bethany the chance to take a more extensive look around. That's when she noticed the full-length mirror standing in the corner. Pushing a few boxes out of the way,

Bethany was able to turn it so she could see herself in the coat before she took it off. Its color matched the lighter strands in her hair, in a style that was both quaint and timeless.

Bethany would gladly purchase the coat if Mrs. Snyder was willing to sell it, but she sensed there was something too special about it to ask. Maybe it was about its history and the people that had borrowed it before. Mrs. Snyder did say it had been a favorite.

She unbuttoned it and placed it beside her purse, to begin working. First, she moved the racks, dividing them between opposite walls of the room, one side for the adult clothing and the other for the children. Bethany then grouped them by categories, rather than by sizes, knowing how much sizing had changed over the years. The mirror was next to be pulled out from the corner with more space around it now to place the chair. Last were the shoes that she separated and lined up against the back wall next to boxes of socks and other accessories that couldn't be hung up.

Bethany stepped back to assess her work, hoping Mrs. Snyder would like the new arrangement. The only place she hadn't touched was a shelf above the shoes that contained a small assortment of backpacks and purses. Loving purses and working for a major purse company, however, she couldn't resist taking a closer look. One never knew what they might find.

A little too high for her to reach, Bethany used the chair as a stepstool to inspect each one. None of them would have likely been expensive, but she was more interested in their designs anyway. She had sketched a few designs of her own, but her supervisor had no interest in seeing them, reminding Bethany her job was only to sell the finished product.

She started to step down off the chair when she noticed what looked to be a misplaced book on the end of the shelf. Maybe at one time, there were used books in the closet for people to borrow. Bethany wasn't sure if a town the size of Snow Valley would have its own library.

There was no title on the front or the spine, so she opened it to see inside. It didn't take any time for her to realize it wasn't a normal book at all, it was the registry Mrs. Snyder had told her about. A quick flip through the pages showed the names of all the people, which items they borrowed, and when.

Bethany stopped to take a longer look at one of the pages. Some of the names had checkmarks beside them and some not. She was pondering what that might mean when she heard footsteps coming and quickly closed the book. It wasn't that she thought Mrs. Snyder would mind her looking, but she didn't want it to appear as if she were prying.

"Bethany, the room looks wonderful! You're already finished?" Mrs. Snyder walked to the middle of the room, admiring all around her.

"I am," she answered, stepping down from the chair and holding out the book. "I also found this on the shelf by the purses, in case you were looking for it."

Mrs. Snyder took the book from Bethany's hands. "Thank you, I was beginning to think I had lost it. For as many years as the closet has been open, it probably doesn't seem like we've helped very many people."

"I don't think it's ever the number that matters." Bethany said, watching Mrs. Snyder open the book and read down some of the entries, herself.

"Here we go," she said, stopping to show Bethany. "About this same time last year, a woman named Angela borrowed the same coat you picked out. The checkmark means she brought it back to us, but if she hadn't, we would simply assume she still needed it."

Bethany took a long look at the entry and smiled. "I'm glad for both of us she didn't." Then feeling a sudden return of anticipation. "Is it time to pick out a Christmas tree yet?"

"Almost," Mrs. Snyder answered, closing the book. "I was coming to tell you I only have the Christmas bulletin left to type, so it shouldn't be too much longer. There's coffee made upstairs if you'd like to help yourself to a cup."

"Is Father Alan still here?" Bethany thought to ask.

Mrs. Snyder gave a gentle laugh. "Unless it's after 4:00 or there's been an emergency, he's always here."

"Okay, I think I'll see if he has time for a short visit while you're finishing up." Bethany picked up the coat and her purse and went with Mrs. Snyder back upstairs. She hoped Father Alan would have some advice on what she should do with the gift.

Approaching his office door, Bethany saw him reading at his desk and lightly knocked. "Father Alan, do you have a minute?"

His head rose with the question. "I have as many as you need," he answered, his full cheeks resting on a beard encircled smile. "Come on in, and tell me what I can do for you."

She walked in and sat down in the same chair across from his desk. "I was wondering if you could tell me more about Nicholas Smith. The inscription on his headstone said that he was a bell maker. I couldn't help but be curious what kind."

Father Alan leaned back and clasped his hands behind his head. "Have you ever heard a real sleigh bell?"

Bethany lifted her shoulders. "I've heard lots of bells before, like the ones on the door of Joe's store. Are those the same thing?"

"No, not like the brass ones Nicholas used to cast. He was a master like no other," Father Alan answered. "You couldn't hear one of his bells without thinking you were hearing something magical. They seemed to have the power to lift anyone's spirits, and many he did."

Bethany was more intrigued than ever. "Where can I hear one?"

Father Alan straightened up in his chair. "That's the difficult part. He sold them faster than he could make them so he was always filling orders. You'd have to find someone who had purchased one from him."

When Bethany didn't respond right away, Father Alan continued. "There's a farm outside of town that's given sleigh rides for years. I have a suspicion they might have some of Nicholas's bells. Maybe sometime you could visit them and find out."

Bethany's mouth twisted in thought, knowing how much she would like to do that, especially if she could also go on a sleigh ride. "I was told his son, Christopher, was in town, but that he was a lot different than his father. 'Crusty' to be exact."

Father Alan chuckled lightly. "That is a pretty accurate description of him."

"Do you have any idea why?" She continued to be curious.

Father Alan's expression softened. "After his mother, Amalie, died, Christopher was like a lost sheep. While Nicholas used his workshop to get through the grief, Christopher wanted nothing to do with making bells until it was too late. He's been coming back every year since Nicholas died, trying to replicate how his father made them. So far, he hasn't been able to figure out what made them special."

Bethany set her eyes on those she knew she could trust. "I don't know what to do, Father Alan."

Those same eyes immediately drew together with concern. "About what?"

"This." She reached into her purse and set the wrapped box on his desk. "Before my mother passed away a few months ago, she asked me to promise I would return this gift to Nicholas. All I had was his name and his address, with specific instructions that it be returned by Christmas Eve. She must have not known when he died."

Father Alan rubbed his hand along his bearded chin. "I gather you're thinking about returning it to Christopher instead."

"It seems to make more sense than burying it next to Nicholas's grave, though I have to admit the thought did cross my mind," Bethany confessed.

"And you don't know what's in the box?" he asked.

Bethany shook her head. "I didn't feel it was my gift to open."

"Then, I think you're right in giving it to Christopher. Maybe he'll be able to tell you why it was important to be returned by Christmas Eve. Who knows, maybe opening the gift will even take some of the crustiness out of him," he said, causing them both to laugh. "But if you do meet him, remember to stand your ground and not take no for an answer."

"I will," she said, putting the box back into her purse.

"I hear a Christmas tree calling our name," Mrs. Snyder's voice practically sang as she entered Father Alan's office, smiling at Bethany. "Are you ready to go?"

Having felt much better after talking to Father Alan, Bethany's mouth easily spread into a matching smile. "I couldn't be more ready."

Chapter Ten

"Where is the Christmas tree lot?" Bethany asked as they scurried out of the church toward the main street sidewalk.

"It's down the block around the corner from The Daily Bread," Mrs. Snyder answered.

Bethany found herself having to walk at a much faster pace to keep up with Mrs. Snyder. "The Daily Bread?"

"That's the name of the café Joe Jr. and his wife, Charlene, own, and they serve some of the best food you'll ever eat. I thought we'd stop in and order some soup after we finished tree shopping."

"So, he owns a café and works at Joe's store?" Bethany asked.

Mrs. Snyder laughed. "Wherever he can stay out of the most trouble, I think. In all seriousness, though, it's nice he can help mind the store when Joe has to be out plowing."

There was no question Bethany had worked up an appetite since breakfast. "Soup sounds wonderful as long as it's my treat," she insisted, before jokingly adding, "Are we in a hurry for a reason?"

Immediate laughter slowed Mrs. Snyder down. "I'm sorry, I didn't realize how fast I was walking. I must be more excited than I realized to get a Christmas tree this year."

The closer they got to The Daily Bread, the stronger the aroma grew from all the cooking and baking going on inside. "If I wasn't already hungry, I would be now," Bethany remarked as they passed by.

"It won't take us long to pick out a tree. The lot is right up there," Mrs. Snyder pointed ahead.

Bethany became as filled with excitement as Mrs. Snyder once she saw the trees lined up in rows from short to tall. Her mind flashed back to when she and her mother had picked out real trees. They weren't near as full or big as these appeared to be, but with lights, tinsel and a few ornaments they never failed to become the most beautiful vision she ever saw. The worst day of the year was always the day they had to take it down.

"Which row should we start looking on?" Bethany asked, her eyes already scanning the snow dusted shapes and sizes.

Mrs. Snyder took Bethany's lead. "How about somewhere in the middle. Joe likes a tree at least as tall as he is, so by the time we add the stand and the star on top, it almost touches the ceiling."

Bethany followed Mrs. Snyder to where the trees were already taller than they were. Surprisingly, there were still plenty to choose from. Some were wide with longer branches while others were narrower and more tapered. Any one of them would have been perfect as far as she was concerned.

"What do you think of this tree?" Mrs. Snyder held one up as straight as she could.

"The trunk seems a bit crooked toward the top, but it has plenty of branches to decorate and it's definitely taller than Joe," Bethany answered after a moment of inspection.

Mrs. Snyder examined the tree herself. "You're right about the trunk. How about I wait here while you see if you can find a better one."

Bethany worked her way down the rest of the row, checking trees on either side of her.

She had almost reached the end when she saw one that appeared to be hiding. Moving the tree in front of it aside, she was able to pull it out and take a closer look. A branch brushed across her nose in the process, leaving the fresh scent of balsam in its path. She closed her eyes and took in an extra breath to forge the scent into her memory.

"You found it, Bethany…the perfect Christmas tree."

Bethany's eyes opened to a beaming Mrs. Snyder right in front of her. "Are you sure? Maybe I should stand it next to the other one before you decide."

Mrs. Snyder's gaze remained fixed on the tree. "I'm sure. I knew as soon as you pulled it out."

By then the man working the lot had finished with another customer and joined them. "You ladies have a good eye for picking out a Christmas tree."

"At least one of us does," Mrs. Snyder said with a wink. "Unfortunately for Bethany, she's been stranded here because of the snowstorm."

"Well, there isn't a better place to be stranded than Snow Valley," he remarked, then turned his attention back to Mrs. Snyder. "When would you like the tree delivered?"

"Sometime this afternoon would be fine. We plan on decorating it later this evening," she answered with a confirming glance at Bethany.

"Will do," the man said, lifting the tree over his shoulder and carrying it away.

For a few seconds, Bethany felt like a piece of her was being carried away with him. She couldn't wait to see it covered in lights and ornaments.

"You ready to head back to The Daily Bread for that homemade soup now?"

Mrs. Snyder's question pulled Bethany from her thoughts. "Nothing could sound more delicious."

Smells to tempt every palate immediately enveloped them as they stepped inside the cafe. Everything from grilled onions, to warm yeast breads, to buttery sweets. Bethany's eyes circled the room from the barstools to the tables. "It's a lot busier in here than I expected with all the snow."

"These are hardy folks. It would take a lot more than snow to keep them away," Mrs. Snyder said, walking over to a small empty table by the window.

They had no more sat down when a waitress approached them with an order pad in hand.

"Hey darlin', it's nice to see you brought along a guest today. Would you like to hear the specials?"

"Charlene, this is Bethany." Mrs. Snyder made the simple introduction with a smile to each of them. "We were wondering what soups were on the menu today."

"It's a pleasure to meet you, Bethany," Charlene responded before answering Mrs. Snyder. "There's the usual tomato or vegetable, plus a new chicken and wild rice

Joe Jr's been working on. Haven't heard any complaints yet."

Mrs. Snyder smiled. "I'll try the chicken and wild rice then."

Bethany couldn't help but notice Charlene studying her while she waited for her to order. "I'll have the chicken and rice as well."

Charlene wrote on the order pad, then looked back up at her. "I don't know why, but there's something about you that looks awfully familiar."

"Maybe it's the coat she's wearing, Charlene. You may be remembering the woman who borrowed it from the clothes closet last year," Mrs. Snyder offered as an explanation.

Charlene's eyebrows narrowed in concentration. "It seems longer ago than that."

"Well, I know you have a better memory than I do," Mrs. Snyder admitted, "but Bethany has never been to Snow Valley before."

"I came here to see Nicholas Smith, not knowing he had already passed away or that I would end up getting stuck in a snowstorm," Bethany revealed.

The lines on Charlene's face only increased. "Hmm...well I'll hurry back with your soup."

Mrs. Snyder looked at Bethany seeming both curious and amused. "That's odd. Never have I seen Charlene so dumbfounded."

Chapter Eleven

"Hi Joe, I'm ready to help," Bethany announced as soon as she entered the store. She listened more carefully to the sound of the bells on the door as she did, wondering if they came anywhere close to sounding like the brass ones Nicholas made.

Joe looked up from behind the counter and grinned. "Already picked out the Christmas tree?"

"The most perfect one on the lot," she answered, her steps still containing the thrill of picking out a real tree. "Then we had a bowl of soup at the café before Mrs. Snyder went home to get the decorations out. Have you had a lot of customers today?"

"Quite a few more than I expected. About sold out of all our batteries and candles," he said, pausing to give her a knowing look. "Though, I have a strong hunch that's not what you're really asking me."

A small sigh preceded Bethany's acknowledgement of the obvious. "So, no Christopher yet."

Joe shook his head. "That doesn't mean he still won't be in. It wouldn't be like him not to show up soon after he got into town."

"And you're sure he got here before they closed the roads?" she checked.

This time Joe nodded.

Bethany set her purse on the counter then looked around at all the shelves. "If you don't mind putting my purse up, I'm going to see what all you have in the store before you put me to work. I may find something I want to buy for myself."

"Take your time now. Joe Jr.'s already been in before he had to be at the café," he said, placing her purse on a shelf behind the register.

"I heard he worked there, too," Bethany said.

Joe chuckled. "Charlene does most of the work running the café. Joe Jr. just likes to experiment with the menu."

Bethany thought back to their lunch. "I have to say his new chicken and wild rice soup was a successful experiment then. It was delicious."

By then she had made her way down the first aisle, taking a mental note of everything she saw. There was such a wide variety of household items, not to mention sections of tools, food, and toys to name in addition.

Bethany paused over a deck of cards, the tops printed with a Norman Rockwell sledding scene, and picked them up. She couldn't remember the last time she had gone sledding or played cards, but she carried them up to the register anyway. Maybe she would get to soon, maybe even with Kenneth.

"Here's something I know I want to buy," she said, carrying the deck over to Joe.

Joe turned his head away from the radio he had been listening to and smiled. "We have a deck of cards just like these at home. Are you sure you want a reminder of all this snow?"

Bethany laughed. "Absolutely. I don't ever want to forget my stay in Snow Valley."

The bells on the front door jingled, causing Bethany's head to snap around. She was ready to help a new customer if nothing else.

A woman started walking toward them, carrying a box not much bigger than the size a pair of shoes would come in. Bethany guessed her to be about the same age as she was.

Joe greeted her with a wave. "Hey Nell, glad to see you didn't have any trouble getting out today."

"Thanks to your expert plowing," Nell replied. "Thought I would bring in the last of this year's ornaments in case someone needed more for their Christmas tree decorating."

"I hope you have more reindeer inside that box. I'm especially running low on those as you can see." Joe pointed to a display at the end of the counter.

Bethany must have missed seeing them amongst the other displays and walked over to take a closer look. On a small rack hung several different shapes of ornaments, all delicately made of leather. There were trees, gingerbread men, reindeer, angels and snowflakes. While each was skillfully tooled with color and detail, she could see why the reindeer was a favorite.

"These are exquisite," she said, turning to look at Nell.

"Nell, this is Bethany, our new friend who's staying with us on account of the snowstorm," Joe began. "Bethany, this is Nell, one of the finest leather craftsmen you'll ever meet."

"It's nice to meet you, Nell." Bethany smiled and returned her focus toward the ornaments. It was then that Joe's words sank in and her head whipped back around. "Wait, you made these?"

Nell nodded as she set the box down and took off the lid. "Before long, it will be time to start next year's designs."

Bethany rejoined Joe and Nell and watched her start removing the ornaments that were inside. "I've never seen this kind of work before. Do you make other items as well?"

"Mostly custom orders, but I've been working on some other ideas to sell here in the store," Nell answered.

"Nell used to make the leather straps for Nicholas's bells," Joe added.

Nell's head popped up from the ornaments to look at Bethany. "Did you know Nicholas, too?"

Bethany was slightly flustered by the question and wished she could answer differently. "No, I'm afraid not, but I've heard a lot about him."

A reminiscent look appeared on Nell's face. "That's too bad. I loved nothing better than seeing his sleigh bells on a piece of leather I had crafted."

"I know he's not here to make them anymore, but aren't there other bells you could use?" Bethany had taken a sincere interest.

Nell drew in a deep breath. "I tried some different ones for a while, like the manufactured ones on the store's door here, but they weren't the same. Nicholas's bells were special in both quality and sound."

Bethany smiled. "So, I've heard. Well, your ornaments are special, too, and I'd like to buy one of each design. That will make five of them."

Nell's mouth opened with surprise. "Please don't feel like you have to buy any."

"These are pieces of art, Nell, and I can't wait to see them hanging on my Christmas tree someday," Bethany assured her like she would an old friend. "Do you mind handing me my purse, Joe?"

As soon as Joe retrieved it off the shelf, Bethany removed enough money to pay for the ornaments and noticed Nell looking intently at her purse.

Her eyes broke away to take the money Bethany handed her and put it in her coat pocket. "Thank you, Bethany. I've never been this close to one of those purses before."

"You know about Touché handbags?" Bethany asked.

"Anything that's made of leather, I do my best to know about," Nell answered. "But Touché isn't a brand seen around here, except maybe in the larger ski resorts. Mind if I take a better look?"

"Not at all. "Bethany moved the purse in front of Nell and watched as she paid attention to every detail of the design. "One of the benefits of working for the company, is getting to choose one to carry."

"Touché puts out a nice product, I'll give them that. Sturdy and structured with classic styling," she finally said after a few more moments.

Bethany laughed. "Maybe you should go to work for them. I think you would do a better job of selling their products than I do."

Nell smiled as she placed the ornaments Bethany had bought into one of Joe's sacks and handed it to her. "I don't think the city life and I would get along very well, but I appreciate the vote of confidence. I hope you enjoy the ornaments as much as I enjoy making them." She then looked at Joe. "I'll see you later. Better get home before the next storm arrives."

Bethany felt a growing sense of anxiety as soon as Nell walked out the door. "Is Nell right, Joe? Is there really another storm coming?"

"There's been some talk, but try not to worry just yet," he answered calmly. "There's just as good a chance it will go north of us, and in the meantime, we have a Christmas tree to decorate."

Bethany managed to relax a little, despite the conflicting emotions, flooding her mind. She knew the best thing to do was to keep busy. "I think I'll start dusting the shelves and sweeping the floor then. Give me a nod if Christopher does show up."

Every time Bethany heard the jingling of bells, she glanced at the door to see who was walking in. Only a couple of times did she see someone who may have passed for crusty. Both times, Joe shook his head to let her know it wasn't him.

It was getting later in the afternoon with fewer customers and little left to do when the bells on the door jingled again. Bethany almost didn't bother to look, but her curiosity was too great. This time when Joe's eyes met hers, he nodded.

Chapter Twelve

Bethany peered through an open shelf as inconspicuously as she could. Of all the different ways she had imagined Christopher looking, none were like this. While she didn't intend to stare, it was difficult not to. Dressed in slacks and a wool topcoat, he could have stepped right out of any office in the city.

"Good to see you, Christopher," Joe greeted. "I was getting concerned, you hadn't made it into the store yet."

"I had a client to meet with first," Christopher started, "but this is the last year you'll be seeing me in Snow Valley, anyway. I've decided to sell the place."

By the expression on Joe's face, he was obviously taken aback. "Are you sure you want to do that? Your family has been a part of this town's history for generations. We know you don't live here now, but it's nice when you come back to visit."

"I think it's pretty obvious, I'm not anything like my family," Christopher replied, his voice more clipped this time.

"You're more like them than you realize, especially your father. Your eyes for one thing, are just like Nicholas's," Joe observed.

Bethany remained frozen in place, mesmerized by the exchange of conversation she was hearing. Christopher's responses made it clear one doesn't have to look crusty to be crusty. That much she had been told about him was true. What she *hadn't* been told about him was that he was handsome, which was also true. More important, however, was realizing if she was ever going to meet him, this was her opportunity.

She caught Joe's eye from her viewing spot and knew he was thinking the same thing. He threw his head back slightly, encouraging her to come out from behind the shelf. Bethany hesitated, then took an extended breath and stepped out into the open.

"Is there something I can find for you?" Bethany asked as if she were a real employee.

Christopher's head spun around to look at her before turning back to Joe.

"It's okay, this is Bethany," Joe gestured toward her with a wink. "She's a visitor to Snow Valley and volunteered to work in the store today."

His gaze returned to Bethany, fully revealing the eyes Joe had referred to, green with hints of gold. "To answer your question, I need a roll of packing tape and a pair of scissors."

Despite feeling her pulse quicken, Bethany managed to form a smile. "I'll be happy to get them for you."

She walked over to where they were located, admonishing herself each step of the way. Why he would be affecting her like this, Bethany didn't know. She had a successful career, dating a successful boyfriend and had dealt with dozens of similar crusty people. She had no reason to be nervous.

Bethany picked up the two items, carried them to the register and set them down. She glanced at Joe then squared her shoulders, understanding it was now or never.

"I couldn't help but overhear the name, Nicholas, mentioned. Is there any chance, it was Nicholas Smith you were talking about?" she asked, emboldened by her new posture.

Christopher had just handed Joe his bank card when he turned to her looking puzzled. "If it was, I'm not sure what that would have to do with you."

Bethany fought to ignore his curtness and maintain her determination. "It's because of Nicholas Smith that I came to Snow Valley. I was sorry to find out he had passed away, and I didn't get to meet him."

Christopher continued his steady gazer. "Is there something you want?"

"No," she pressed, trying not to be insulted. "I came here for my mother."

Christopher put the card back into his wallet and picked up the sack Joe had put his items in. "I doubt I would know anything about your mother, and I really don't have any more time to waste."

Bethany watched him turn toward the door and knew she had to stop him. "But I have an important question I'm hoping you can answer, plus a gift that was supposed to be returned to your father. Besides, you're not the only one who doesn't have time to waste. I have to drive back to the city tomorrow."

For the first time, Christopher seemed slightly amused. "Have you not seen the latest weather forecast? It's getting ready to dump as many inches of snow as it did yesterday, if not more. No one will be traveling anywhere tomorrow."

"If that's the case then you can meet me for coffee at The Daily Bread since, of course, we'll both be here."

"Maybe I don't drink coffee."

"I'm betting you do," Bethany challenged him. This time she looked straight into his eyes, no longer feeling any intimidation.

Christopher looked away, as if debating how to respond.

"I'll promise never to bother you again." Bethany upped the ante with her best hand. It was now his decision to raise or fold.

"9:00," he finally said, lifting his chin.

Bethany crossed her arms and did the same. "Will you promise?"

By then, Christopher was well on his way out of the store, but his answer was loud and clear. "I don't make promises lightly."

"Neither do I," Bethany half-hollered behind him. She waited until the door was closed and the bells had quieted before she turned to look wide-eyed at Joe. The grin he wore made her burst out laughing. "Is he always that exasperating?"

Joe laughed along with her. "I'm pretty sure Christopher Smith just met his match and he doesn't even know it."

As entertaining as the sparring of wills had been, reality swept into her thoughts. If she were to meet with Christopher and give him the gift, it would be because she was unable to get back to the city and back to Kenneth. That would mean a canceled trip to the Caribbean, possibly even a canceled boyfriend. Bethany's mind continued to play tug-o-war with her emotions, neither side prepared to give up any ground.

"I think we can close up a little early. Are you ready to go home?" Joe asked, unaware of the mental battle he was interrupting.

Home...though not hers, it was the one where Mrs. Snyder was waiting for them. Nothing could have sounded more comforting to Bethany. "Yes, I am."

Joe started turning off lights, getting ready to lock up. "Well, there's no telling what Mrs. Snyder has in store for us. I haven't seen her so happy about decorating a Christmas tree in a long while."

Bethany smiled. "She's not the only one, Joe."

After picking up the sack of ornaments and the deck of cards she had purchased, they were soon inside Joe's pickup and on their way. The soft rumble of the truck's engine filled her with a sense of peace, the opposite result of her meeting with Christopher. So, what if he was handsome. It was more important what kind of heart he had, and at that moment, she wasn't sure he had one.

Watching snowflakes begin to accumulate on the windshield, she no longer had to wonder whether or not it was going to snow again. The only question was...how much?

Chapter Thirteen

Joe and Bethany walked into the house to the mouth-watering smell of something sizzling on top of the stove. Mrs. Snyder was quick to poke her head around from the kitchen. "By the time Joe gets a fire going, dinner should be ready."

With a smile, Bethany took off her coat and looked around the room. The tree was in its stand in front of the large picture window with boxes of decorations stacked next it, waiting to be opened. She walked over to take a deep breath of its fresh scented needles, wishing she could bottle it somehow. While Bethany still hoped she and Kenneth would soon be walking barefoot on sun-kissed sand, she didn't regret her trip to Snow Valley for one moment.

"Is everything all right, Bethany?"

Bethany turned to see the look that accompanied Mrs. Snyder's question, unaware of how long she had been lost in thought. She hurried to dispel any concern and reached out to feel one of the branches. "I can't seem to get enough of this tree is all."

"Well, let's eat while dinner is good and hot, and we'll get busy decorating it," Mrs. Snyder said.

It was then that Bethany saw the platter of fried chicken and bowls of gravy, mashed potatoes, and green beans that had been set on the table. The vision embodied the very definition of comfort food.

Joe and Bethany took a seat while Mrs. Snyder lit the candle inside the holly covered centerpiece. "There's nothing like a candle to make any occasion feel more festive, especially this time of year."

Bethany couldn't have agreed more as she watched the flame, flicker to life.

"Mind if I say grace?" Joe asked.

"Not at all." Bethany reached out to clasp hands with the both of them and listen to Joe's words of thanksgiving.

"…and last but not least, we thank you for bringing our guest, Bethany, into our home. May we be as great a blessing to her as she has been to us. Amen," he ended the prayer.

The mentioning of her name produced a sensation that almost took Bethany's breath away. There was no denying the connection she felt to this town and to these people, even if she didn't understand why.

While they passed the bowls of food around, Joe proceeded to tell the story about meeting Christopher in a way that was much more humorous than Bethany remembered. By the end of it, they were all laughing. "You'd have been proud of this girl, Mrs. Snyder."

"I'm sure I would have," she said, still laughing.

Remnants of a grin lingered as Bethany began to eat. "Father Alan did tell me not to take no for an answer."

"And, *no*, you didn't," Joe emphasized.

Bethany's next few minutes were spent enjoying her food until she had finished everything on her plate. "This dinner was so good, Mrs. Snyder, I had a hard time, slowing down."

"I'm sure you worked up an appetite, organizing the clothes closet and helping out at the store," Mrs. Snyder responded. "I just hope you left room for a bit of dessert. It's tradition for us to have a cup of homemade eggnog after decorating the tree."

"I daresay it's the best you'll ever taste, too," Joe added.

"Oh, I always have room for dessert." Bethany stood up from her chair to start collecting the plates. "And the faster I get these dishes washed, the faster we can have some."

Mrs. Snyder picked up the remaining dishes and followed Bethany into the kitchen. "I will help you."

"You have eggnog to make, remember. I'll have them done in no time." she said, already filling the sink with hot, sudsy water.

Mrs. Snyder gave in with a smile and started pulling ingredients out of the refrigerator and setting them on the counter.

Bethany caught glimpses of her beating the eggs, then adding sugar, milk, and cream into a pan and whisking it all together over the burner. Last, came the vanilla and spices that infused the kitchen with a warm, sweet aroma. Such simple ingredients for something destined to be so good. She couldn't wait to taste it.

"All it needs is time to chill in the refrigerator and it should be ready when we are," Mrs. Snyder said, picking up an extra dish towel to finish drying the last few pots and pans. "Now, let's go decorate us a tree."

Joe had all the light strands separated and ready to hang. Starting from the base of the tree, Bethany helped to wind them throughout the branches, adding one strand at a time until the entire tree was aglow with light. She stepped back to gaze at it, already thinking it looked beautiful.

"And for the best part." Mrs. Snyder took the top off the largest box to reveal rows and layers of ornaments. "Some of these are from our childhood and some are ones I've made. Most of them I've just collected through the years."

Bethany picked up a stuffed felt Santa with a red-sequined hat, she was sure Mrs. Snyder must have made and hung it first. They continued to take turns, bringing the tree to life with memories of every size and kind.

"I can't believe we found room for all of these," Joe teased when they were about done.

"Joe Snyder, you know you can never have too many ornaments," Mrs. Snyder scolded.

"That reminds me of something. I'll be right back." Bethany ran to the bedroom and returned with her hands behind her back. "I met Nell at the store today and bought some of her ornaments." She then held out the angel in front of her to give to Mrs. Snyder. "As soon as I saw this, I knew I wanted you to have it."

Mrs. Snyder gazed thoughtfully as she took the angel into her hand. "Thank you, Bethany, it's lovely. That Nell is so talented. Maybe you'll have a chance to visit her shop that's over by the Christmas tree lot." She then looked back at the tree. "Where should I hang it?"

Bethany looked alongside her. "Anywhere would be fine, but how about next to the snowflake? I'd like to think it was an angel who guided me safely back here in the snow, until Joe came along of course."

"Then that is the perfect place," Mrs. Snyder reached up and placed it on the branch right above the snowflake. "There's only one more thing left to do."

That was all the prompting Joe needed to open a smaller box and pull out a shiny gold star. Bethany was inspired to watch him carefully set it in its place of honor, at the very tip-top. It truly was a special Christmas tree.

"You two sit down now, while I get the eggnog," Mrs. Snyder said, heading for the kitchen.

Bethany sat on the sofa as Joe put on another album of Christmas music. She considered asking him if he had received any updates on the weather, then decided against it. If there was going to be another snowstorm, there was nothing she could do to stop it.

Mrs. Snyder brought in a tray with three cups and set it on the coffee table. "Shall we make a toast?"

Each of them took a cup and raised it, with Joe speaking up first. "To a very Merry Christmas."

Mrs. Snyder's followed next. "To Bethany and the gift of new friends."

Inhaling a breath of gratitude, Bethany made hers. "To two of the nicest people I've ever met, who welcomed me into their home like family."

After a clink between cups, Bethany took a drink of the creamy beverage that had been sprinkled with extra spice.

The eggnog she was used to drinking didn't come close to being this good. She took her time between each sip, not wanting to finish it too quickly.

Joe kept them laughing with jokes and stories until he finally pushed himself up from the chair. "As much as I hate to call it a night, there's no telling what I may be waking up to in the morning." He started to walk off then paused. "But I do have to say, you ladies picked out a nice tree."

Bethany grinned. "I'm not sure it wasn't the tree that picked us out, Joe."

She turned her attention back to Mrs. Snyder. "We've had such a busy day, I'll be fine if you want to call it a night, too. I think I'll sit and admire the tree a while longer."

"There's still a small fire going. I think admiring our beautiful tree would be a wonderful way to top off the day." Mrs. Snyder grabbed a blanket to share between them.

Bethany curled her feet underneath her, remembering always wanting to sleep next to the Christmas tree when she was growing up, and the occasional times her mother would let her. The memory caused moisture to fill her eyes.

"Bethany, what is it?" Mrs. Snyder reached over with her hand.

Her touch was all it took for the levy to break and tears begin to flow. Unable to wipe them away fast enough, Mrs. Snyder hurried to grab a box of tissues.

Bethany took extra out to dry her face. "What's wrong with me, that I don't even know why I'm crying?"

"You've been through more than you realize. Didn't you just lose your mother a few months ago?"

Bethany could only nod.

"It's been many years since I lost mine and I still miss her greatly. Why do you think I make blueberry muffins all the time?"

"Because that's what your mother used to do?" Bethany answered with a question of her own.

This time it was Mrs. Snyder's turn to nod. "I don't mean to pry, but is your father gone as well?"

Bethany waited for her next breath. "Yes, though I never knew him. He left my mother before I was born."

"That must have been hard on you both."

"It was for the best. My mother thought the news he was going to be a father would change him, but it only made him make more promises he couldn't keep."

Mrs. Snyder wrapped an arm around Bethany and held her close. For a quiet length of time, the crackling of a fire left to burn on its own, was all that could be heard.

Chapter Fourteen

Without looking out the window the next morning, Bethany already knew she wasn't going to be driving back to the city. She had heard Joe leave the house in the middle of the night, though it wasn't as if he had awakened her. Worrying about what she may have to tell Kenneth had kept her up most of the night.

Bethany looked at her phone to check the time, surprised it was already 7:00 a.m. and Kenneth hadn't called yet. Not wanting to stay in bed any longer, she tied her robe around her, went to the window, and pulled back the curtain. There was no question the new snowfall was as deep as the one before.

The fresh smell of coffee soon lured Bethany from the bedroom, where she saw Mrs. Snyder standing next to the percolator, almost as if she were watching it brew.

"Good morning," she said, entering the kitchen.

Mrs. Snyder turned around with a quick smile. "Good morning. You caught me finishing up my percolator prayers."

"Percolator prayers?" Bethany repeated, trying not to look too confused.

Mrs. Snyder's smile broadened into a laugh. "It must sound pretty silly."

Bethany let herself join in, feeling her mood lighten. "I don't think it sounds silly at all. I've just never heard of them."

"Years ago, I discovered that in the amount of time it took for the coffee to percolate, I can count all my blessings and say prayers for everyone I know that needs them," she explained while pulling two cups from the cabinet.

Bethany thought about her own blessings as she watched Mrs. Snyder pour the coffee and set the cups on the table. She knew she didn't count hers near often enough.

"You must be awfully disappointed about the weather," Mrs. Snyder spoke again more hesitantly after they sat down. "Being snowbound in Snow Valley is far from the vacation you'd been dreaming about. Have you talked to Kenneth?"

Bethany shook her head. "I have a feeling he's waiting for me to call him."

"And you haven't because…?" Mrs. Snyder's eyebrows rose with the question.

"He's going to blame me for messing up our plans, and the truth is, he wouldn't be wrong," she answered.

Mrs. Snyder's gentle eyes rested on Bethany's. "Storms of all kinds are bound to happen in life, and that includes snowstorms. If he's deserving of you, he'll be by your side, facing them together."

Bethany was giving Mrs. Snyder's words a chance to sink in when she heard her phone ringing from the bedroom. Instead of running to answer it, however, she continued to drink her coffee. The entire time she and

Kenneth had been dating, she felt like the one who didn't deserve him. The thought it could be the other way around never occurred to her.

"I suppose I should call him back," she said.

Mrs. Snyder gave her a nod of understanding. "The sooner the better, I'm afraid."

Bethany went to the bedroom and picked up her phone, still trying to convince herself this wasn't her fault. She held her breath as she pushed his number.

"Why didn't you answer a minute ago?" Kenneth's voice blurted within the first ring.

"I was in another room and didn't have my phone with me."

"Are you getting ready to leave?"

"I can't, Kenneth. The roads are still closed."

"What are you talking about?"

"I figured you had seen the weather. Another big snowstorm hit here last night."

"So, I'm just supposed to cancel our trip?"

Bethany closed her eyes to keep her voice steady. "I'm sorry, Kenneth, I don't know what other choice we have. Maybe we can reschedule it for later."

"Don't worry, there won't be a later."

The finality of his words stung. Bethany walked back into the kitchen, fighting back tears as she spoke. "I don't think Kenneth ever wants to see me again."

Mrs. Snyder stood up and held Bethany in her arms. "Give him a little time to get over it. I'm sure he'll come around."

"But what if he doesn't?"

"Try not to worry about that today. It may not be much of a consolation, but know that all of Snow Valley is glad you're here, and for however long you stay, our home is your home."

Bethany wiped away the few tears that had escaped and looked from the Christmas tree to Mrs. Snyder. "You have no idea how happy that makes me, because this does feel like home."

Mrs. Snyder's eyes shone as if she were fighting back tears of her own. "Why don't I fix us some breakfast, then we can meet later at the church to find you a few more clothes."

Bethany started to nod before she suddenly remembered. "I told Christopher I'd meet him at the café at 9:00 if I was still in town."

"Then I'll fix something extra quick and have it on the table by the time you get dressed," Mrs. Snyder said.

She went to her room, hoping Christopher hadn't forgotten. By the time Bethany returned to the kitchen, there was a plate of sugar-dusted French toast, waiting for her on the table. She was used to grabbing breakfast on the run if she ate at all. What she wasn't used to, was taking time to enjoy it. Her next glance at the clock revealed she only had fifteen minutes left to get to the café.

"I'd be glad to drive you," Mrs. Snyder offered.

"Thank you, but a quick walk will do me good this morning. See you at the church in a bit," Bethany said as she rushed out the door.

Hurrying in snow boots was harder than she thought, and Bethany was both breathless and late, by the time she entered The Daily Bread. Her eyes immediately began to scan the room for Christopher, shifting quickly from table to table, then barstool to barstool along the counter. He wasn't anywhere inside the café that she could see. Surely, he knew the road was closed again and she would be there.

For a moment, Bethany wondered if Christopher might be running late as well, but knew it wasn't likely. He came across as the type that either arrived on time or not all. She walked to an empty stool at the counter and sat down to wait for Charlene to come by. Asking her would be the easiest way to find out.

The moment came faster than Bethany expected as Charlene seemed to fly down the counter toward her with a pot of coffee in her hand. "Morning Darlin'," she greeted with a smile as she placed a cup in front of her and started pouring. "I'm sorry about all the new snow, but I'm glad to see you again. What can I get for you?"

Despite the way the morning had gone with Kenneth, Bethany couldn't help but respond with a smile of her own. "Thank you, Charlene. Just coffee will do for now."

"It's on the house then. Holler if you change your mind," she said, already moving on down the counter to refill cups and take more orders.

Bethany realized she had hesitated a second too long. While hollering wasn't her style, she raised her arm and waved to get Charlene's attention.

Charlene had her pen and pad in hand when she returned. "Did you decide you were hungry?"

Bethany shook her head. "I forgot to ask if you had seen Christopher Smith in the café this morning?"

"Sure did. Sat over at the corner table by the window," she said with a nod in that direction. "He hadn't been gone but a few minutes before you got here."

"Thanks, Charlene." Bethany watched her scurry back to work, then took a final gulp from her cup, and got down from the stool. At least Christopher had shown up without promising he would, but he could have waited just a little longer.

Bethany stepped back out onto the sidewalk and started walking. Where she was going, she didn't know. It was too early to meet Mrs. Snyder at the church and Joe Jr. was working the store until Joe finished plowing. Then she remembered Mrs. Snyder mentioning that Nell had her own shop near the Christmas tree lot.

She turned and headed in that direction, noticing there were but a few trees remaining. It made her happy, knowing it meant more real trees were being decorated for Christmas. She kept an eye out for Nell's shop, but it wasn't until Bethany spied a small tree in a window decorated with leather ornaments that she knew she had found it.

With no lights on inside, Bethany assumed Nell wasn't there. She walked up next to the door and looked through the glass to make sure. Seeing all of Nell's tools and supplies laid out on the tables stirred up a bit of envy inside her. Nell was lucky to be doing something she loved and was good at. While Bethany considered herself good at her job, she couldn't say she loved it. Seeing all the pieces of leather lying about reminded her of what her dream had once been.

Bethany was just turning to leave when a familiar truck pulled up beside her and rolled down its window.

"You look like someone I know. Why don't you hop in?" Joe teased as he waved her over.

She laughed as she opened the door stepped up to the seat. "I guess you're done plowing for the day?"

"Dare say I am," he answered. "I figured you might still be at the café talking to a certain someone."

Bethany released a sigh. "Charlene said he was there, but I was a few minutes late so he left before I had the chance."

Joe tapped his chin and gave her a sly grin. "I think it's time you pay Christopher Smith a visit."

Chapter Fifteen

Bethany felt a surprising sense of calm when she and Joe reached the end of Oaktree Lane and stopped in front of Christopher's house. Instead of appearing dark and abandoned like it had before, the drifts of snow banked around its edges, along with the swirls of smoke rising from the chimney made it look welcoming.

"I shouldn't be very long, Joe," she said, deciding to leave the gift in her purse until the right moment presented itself.

"Take all the time you need. You know I'll be right here waiting for you."

Bethany gave him an extended smile. "I know."

She exited the truck and made her way up the steps to knock on the front door. When there was no answer, Bethany lifted her chin and knocked again, remembering Father Alan's words not to take no for an answer. If he thought he could simply ignore her, he had another thing coming. This time the door opened, and Bethany came face to face with the man she determined had stood her up.

Christopher's eyebrows rose when he saw her. "What can I do for you?"

"You were supposed to meet me for coffee this morning. When I arrived at the cafe, however, Charlene told me you had already left."

"When you weren't there by 9:00, I figured you must have made it back to the city."

Bethany stared at him in disbelief. "Well, I didn't have the phone number to the North Pole to hire Santa's reindeers or I would have. I was only a few minutes late."

"Have you never heard the saying, 'If you're early, you're on time; if you're on time you're late.' That means you were extra late, and maybe I had better things to do during those few minutes," he countered.

That was all it took for Bethany's patience to reach its threshold. "You don't think *I* had better things to do? If it weren't for a promise I made to my mother, I would be on my way to the Caribbean today. Instead, here I am, stuck in the snow, doing my best to be nice to the one person who might be able to help me, but who's been nothing but crusty and ill-humored."

Christopher eyed her more intensely "A promise to your mother, huh…and just crusty and ill-humored?"

Bethany began holding up one finger at a time. "How about rude, selfish, dull, egotistical…"

He threw up his hand to stop her. "I think I've got the idea."

"The only reason I even came to Snow Valley was because I promised to return a gift to your father by Christmas Eve. Since that's no longer possible, I think you should have it." Aside from her words of frustration, Bethany felt a tug of compassion for him, knowing they both had suffered losses."

Christopher turned his gaze away from her for a long moment. When it returned, his expression was more subdued. "You can keep it. I don't have any use for gifts right now."

"But you don't even know what it is. Aren't you the least bit curious?" Bethany was careful to tread lightly, not wanting to give up.

"Not anymore. I'm sorry if I've wasted your time, and I do mean that." His usual brusqueness had diminished, allowing a hint of sincerity to lace his words.

Bethany decided it was worth trying an old adage of her mother's and held out her hand for him to shake. "Well, I never consider meeting a new friend a waste of time."

Christopher had already taken a step backward, but paused. His eyes shifted from Bethany to her extended arm. Hesitating slightly, he reached out to shake it, then continued backing away and closed the door.

Seeing him again didn't turn out quite as Bethany hoped, but she sensed a crack in his defenses that made her unwilling to give up on him just yet. She returned to the truck thinking the old adage may be right, that you do catch more flies with honey.

"Should I ask how it went?" Joe asked as soon as she was back in the front seat.

Bethany's shoulders lifted in a shrug. "He doesn't want the gift."

Joe began driving back toward town. "You know you did your best."

Bethany wanted to believe Joe's words, but she couldn't shake the feeling she had failed her mission. "Christopher seems so miserable here, I'm not surprised he's selling the place. I'm more surprised he hadn't done it sooner."

Joe voiced a soft grunt. "In case you couldn't tell, he's a tad bit on the stubborn side. He's been trying for years to make up for being late."

"Late for what?" she questioned with a frown.

Joe's face was more serious when he glanced at her to answer. "I think that's something Christopher himself would have to explain."

"Well, whatever it was only seemed to make him less forgiving of anyone else being late. Thank you for taking me to see him," Bethany said, managing to shake off her frustration.

"You're welcome. Where can I take you now?"

"How about the church? Mrs. Snyder and I are going to look for a few more things to borrow from the clothes closet."

"To the church it is then," Joe said, turning the truck back toward town.

Bethany started to get out as soon as he pulled up but paused when a picture of Nell's shop flashed through her mind. "Do you mind if I ask a favor, Joe, even though I hate to since you've already done so much for me."

"That's not the way it works around here," he said with a wink. "What can I do for you?"

"Would you mind bringing home one of those sketch pads I saw in the store, along with a couple of pencils? That is, as long as you let me know how much I owe you for them."

"Yes, ma'am. An order for one sketch pad and a couple of pencils it is."

She closed the door and waved, then started walking alongside the church to where the cemetery and the entrance to the offices were. Instead of going right in, however, Bethany found herself drawn to Nicholas's gravesite, fixing her eyes again on his epitaph.

"The Bell Maker," she read aloud. "I don't know what happened, Nicholas, but I hope somewhere buried inside your son is another bell maker."

Bethany immediately looked around to make sure no one had heard her talking to a granite headstone, although she was sure many others had done the same thing. It wasn't like she expected it to talk back to her.

When she entered the building, the hallway had been lined with boxes of wreaths, garlands and poinsettia plants. Bethany followed the trail, leading toward the sanctuary where she began to hear voices mingled with laughter. She smiled, recognizing one of them as Mrs. Snyder's.

"Hi," she said as she came through the doorway.

Mrs. Snyder, plus two other women, all turned to look at her. "You're just in time, Bethany. Come on in."

Bethany walked up the aisle to join them. The shorter of the women immediately took hold of her hands. "I'm Doris, it's so nice to meet you."

"And I'm Kathryn," the other woman introduced herself. "Gwen told us about your unfortunate snowstorm adventure, but I'm a firm believer something good will come out of it. You just wait and see."

Bethany shot Mrs. Snyder a grin before responding to them. It was nice to learn what her given name was. "I'm glad to meet both of you, too."

"Doris and Kathryn are in charge of the hanging of the greens," Mrs. Snyder explained.

"We would love for you to help us." Doris's enthusiasm filled each of her words.

"You are staying through Christmas, aren't you?" Kathryn asked.

Bethany searched Mrs. Snyder's face.

"Joe and I would love nothing more than for you to stay, but we understand if you have to get back to the city," she said, exposing a look of wistfulness.

The truth was she had nothing to go back to, no family, and no friends that hadn't already made plans for the holidays. It appeared, no Kenneth either. She had already taken vacation time from work until after the New Year.

"I'll have to see how things work out, but I would love to help you decorate," she answered them.

"How wonderful," Doris gushed with appreciation. "We start at 10:00 tomorrow morning.

Mrs. Snyder looped her arm through Bethany's to begin guiding her out of the sanctuary. "In the meantime, we need to find her some more clothes to wear."

"See you tomorrow," Bethany said.

Once they were out of danger of being heard, Mrs. Snyder spoke again. "I apologize if they were a bit overwhelming. They really do mean well."

Bethany laughed. "No apology necessary, and now I know your first name. Would you prefer I call you Gwen instead of Mrs. Snyder?"

"You call me anything you'd like," Mrs. Snyder said with a laugh of her own. She then took her key and unlocked the door to the clothes closet. "Finally, I have a chance to hear about your meeting with Christopher. Sit down and tell me how it went before we start searching the racks."

"There's not too much to tell except that he's undoubtedly a grumpy sort who couldn't wait a few extra minutes and left the cafe before I even got there. When Joe drove me to his house, he wasn't at all interested in taking the gift I was supposed to return to his father," Bethany explained before drawing another, long breath. "I'm still figuring out what to do next, but may I ask you something?"

Mrs. Snyder focused her attention on Bethany. "Of course, you may."

Bethany searched her face. "Did you really mean what you said, that you and Joe would love to have me stay here for Christmas?"

The question seemed to make Mrs. Snyder's entire face smile. "Oh Bethany, with all my heart."

Chapter Sixteen

With a sack full of clothes and a dress Mrs. Snyder thought would be perfect for her to wear on Christmas Eve, Bethany led the way out of the clothes closet, both of them still laughing.

"Do you really think Joe will wear it? I mean, it's definitely jolly," Bethany paused to question.

Mrs. Snyder rolled her eyes and grinned. "A tie with a Santa Claus, surrounded in candy canes? Oh, he'll wear it all right. It's too bad he doesn't have a sweater to match it. There's nothing Joe likes better than making people smile, especially the children."

Bethany noticed Mrs. Snyder's voice softening with her last few words. She wouldn't dream of prying into why she and Joe didn't have any children of their own, but there was no doubt they would have made wonderful parents.

"If you don't mind stopping at the grocery store on the way home, I thought I'd make spaghetti and meatballs for our dinner tonight." Bethany suggested on their way back up the stairs.

"That's one of our favorite dinners, but I don't want you to feel like you have to cook for us, Bethany," Mrs. Snyder said.

Bethany turned toward Mrs. Snyder when they reached the top. "I enjoy being in the kitchen, though you can help chop the onions, if you'd like."

"Sounds like someone is cooking up something...literally." Father Alan walked out of his office, chuckling.

"Just tonight's dinner," Mrs. Snyder said before her face brightened. "Why don't you join us?"

"Please, Father Alan," Bethany's eyebrows rose in expectation. "I think you'll like the spaghetti and meatballs I'm fixing."

Father Alan looked at each of them. "I've never been able to say no to good food, and I have a feeling I would never be able to say no to you two either."

"Great! I'll have Joe pick you up as soon as he closes the store," Mrs. Snyder confirmed. "We're on our way out, since there's nothing else on the calendar for today. I can only say it's going to be an extra special hanging of the greens in the morning with Bethany helping us."

Father Alan's eyes were hopeful as he looked at Bethany. "Does that mean you may be staying in Snow Valley for Christmas after all?"

Bethany nodded then turned her gaze to Mrs. Snyder. "I'm looking forward to it," she answered, producing a smile between them.

"Best be careful, or Doris and Kathryn will have you dressed in a robe and singing in the choir next," Father Alan warned.

Mrs. Snyder laughed as she opened the door to leave. "You're right about that. We'll see you this evening."

"Bye, Father Alan," Bethany added on their way out.

They were walking toward the car when Mrs. Snyder's steps slowed. "Are you sure about staying? I don't want you to feel like you've been pressured into it."

Bethany stopped to give her a look of unwavering assurance. "Right now, Mrs. Snyder, it's the *only* thing I'm sure of."

Mrs. Snyder reached an arm around Bethany's shoulders for a quick but affirming hug. "Why don't we stop in the café and see Charlene before we get what we need for dinner. She makes a delicious peppermint hot chocolate, complete with a candy cane."

"That sounds like the perfect way to celebrate Joe's new tie," Bethany said, causing them to giggle.

From the looks of the café as they pulled up, it wasn't as busy as the other times Bethany had been there. They ended up choosing the same table they had sat at the day before, right next to the window.

Bethany couldn't keep her eyes from peering out the glass, adorned with both real snow and the artificial kind that had been sprayed on in an array of holiday shapes and greetings. "The snow is still so beautiful to look at. I wonder if it will last until Christmas."

"According to Joe Jr., we'll have a fresh blanket by then," a new voice responded.

Bethany turned in time to see Charlene placing mugs of peppermint hot chocolate in front of them. "How did you know this is what we were going to order?"

"You'll soon learn she can practically read minds," Mrs. Snyder answered with a playful glance at her friend.

Charlene laughed as she sat at the table to join them. "Since we tend to be creatures of habit, it's not as hard as you think. Gwen has never come to the café at this time of day and this close to Christmas when she hasn't wanted a peppermint hot chocolate."

Bethany stirred hers with the candy cane and took a long sip. "I can understand why. It's delicious."

"Thank you," Charlene said, with a lingering smile. "Were you able to talk to Christopher yet?"

Bethany had a difficult time keeping her frustration to herself. "Yes, but it didn't do much good. He's not exactly the friendly type."

Charlene's eyebrows lifted knowingly. "If you want to try again, be here at his usual time in the morning, 8:00 sharp."

"I'll keep that in mind," Bethany said, already entertaining the thought she should try at least one more time to get through to him.

"Hey everyone."

"Hi, Nell," Mrs. Snyder said.

Bethany thought the voice sounded familiar and looked up to see her standing by the table next to Charlene. "I walked by your shop earlier, but you weren't there."

"Sorry I missed you. I had to run some errands for Mom here or I would have been."

"Which I owe you a big thank you for." Charlene looked up to Nell with a smile.

Bethany's eyes shifted between the two of them, realizing how similar their traits were. "So, you are mother and daughter, which makes Joe Jr…"

"My dad," Nell chimed in.

"It may be hard to believe, but many of us who grew up in Snow Valley are still here," Mrs. Snyder said.

"There's a lot of love in this community to convince people to want to stay. I can't imagine a better place to live, though I understand it sometimes takes leaving to appreciate it." Charlene winked at her daughter as she finished.

"That will have to be a story for another day, Mom. We need to get these supplies put away," Nell reminded her.

Charlene stood up. "Duty calls. You two enjoy the rest of your day."

Bethany waved good-bye at Nell as they walked away and with one more tip of her mug, her hot chocolate was all gone.

"You really think we'll get more snow for Christmas?" Bethany asked once they were in the car on the way to the store.

"Joe Jr's predictions have been right more often than any weather forecaster," Mrs. Snyder answered. "He says nature and the Farmer's Almanac are the best indicators of the weather, not fancy radar systems."

Bethany smiled. "I'd be okay if it does." She then reflected on finding out Nell was Charlene and Joe Jr.'s daughter. "Nell looks to be about my age."

"She turned twenty-eight this year," Mrs. Snyder offered while turning into a parking spot.

"That's funny. She's exactly my age then," Bethany said.

Mrs. Snyder turned off the engine and gave Bethany a studied look. Her face seemed to grow slightly pale, causing Bethany some concern. "Are you feeling okay, Mrs. Snyder? We can go home so you can rest, and I'll come back on my own for the ingredients."

"No, I'll be fine, I probably just had too many sweets today," Mrs. Snyder reasoned the concern away and opened her door. "Let's go get what we need for those wonderful sounding spaghetti and meatballs."

Chapter Seventeen

Bethany prepared the sauce as soon as they got home, so it would have the rest of the afternoon to simmer and season before Joe and Father Alan arrived. When it came time for her and Mrs. Snyder to set the table and finish getting the rest of the meal ready, she found herself unable to resist humming Christmas carols.

"You hum nicely," Mrs. Snyder said.

Bethany looked at her and smiled. "Thank you, if only I could sing as well."

"I bet you do. What is your favorite carol to sing?" Mrs. Snyder asked.

That was a difficult question since Bethany loved them all. She thought for a moment before finally answering, "I think it might be "Angels We Have Heard on High," mostly because I love to belt out the chorus."

"Angels we have heard on high…" Mrs. Snyder began singing.

Bethany didn't hesitate to join in. "Sweetly singing o'er the plains...."

They continued singing the rest of the verses, ending with a robust, "Glo…ria, in excelsis Deo."

"Why you'd think Christmas was coming," Father Alan's voice resonated from the living room.

Bethany and Mrs. Snyder laughed as they stepped into the kitchen doorway, not having heard him and Joe walk into the house.

"Whatever made you think that, Father Alan?" Mrs. Snyder teased.

Father Alan smiled. "Oh, the wreath on the door and the beautiful Christmas tree were my first clues, but it wasn't until I heard that joyous singing that I knew for sure. Our choir sure could use a voice like yours, Bethany."

"It is lovely, isn't it," Mrs. Snyder glanced at her in warm agreement.

Joe then held up a sack he held in his hand. "I believe this is for you, Bethany."

Bethany walked over to take it and pulled out the sketchpad and pencils. "Thank you, Joe."

"Are you an artist?" Father Alan asked.

"Not really. I just enjoy sketching out some ideas I have." She moved next to the tree to touch the angel ornament she had bought from Nell. "This is what a real artist does."

"Well, I happen to think good cooking classifies as art, and by the smell of your spaghetti and meatballs, I would say you are, too," Father Alan declared.

"Speaking of cooking, dinner is ready, so you two can set yourselves down in a chair while Bethany and I serve it," Mrs. Snyder said.

Joe was already heading in that direction. "You don't have to tell me twice."

Bethany joined Mrs. Snyder back in the kitchen to place the sauce and meatballs over a large platter of spaghetti noodles. Adding a topping of parmesan cheese, she then set it in the middle of the table. Mrs. Snyder followed behind her with a bowl of salad and a tray of buttered garlic toast.

"Now, this is what I call a feast," Father Alan remarked after saying the blessing.

"I hope it tastes worthy of being called one," Bethany chuckled.

The table was quiet as they all served themselves and began to eat. "This is more than worthy, Bethany," Mrs. Snyder was the first to speak up.

Nods of agreement came from Joe and Father Alan, as they continued being busy enjoying the meal.

Joe soon patted his stomach. "I don't think I'll need to eat for another week."

"You know better than to have seconds, Joe Snyder," Mrs. Snyder teasingly scolded.

He smiled. "Something this good, it's too hard not to. I think the only remedy for being this full is a game of rummy."

"You can get the cards out and we'll play as soon as we take care of the dishes," Mrs. Snyder suggested.

Bethany rinsed off the plates Father Alan brought to the sink while Mrs. Snyder put away the leftover food. In a matter of minutes, they were back at the table ready to play. She recognized the decks of cards Joe laid down.

"You really do have cards like the ones I bought from your store," she said.

"Only these have been around for over forty years," he responded with a glowing look at Mrs. Snyder.

"Joe gave me them to me after the first time we went sledding together," Mrs. Snyder explained, "claiming we looked like that boy and girl."

"Used to, anyway," Joe winked. "When I saw I could order some to sell at the store, how could I resist?"

After several rounds, it looked like Joe was going to win until Father Alan pulled ahead on the last round. "Seems like a perfect time to end the game," he said, making everyone laugh. "But as enjoyable as this has been, I should probably be heading home to prepare for tomorrow. It's a big day with the hanging of the greens."

Bethany watched as he and Joe started to stand and jumped up from her chair. "I need to do something before you leave, if that's okay. I promise it won't take long."

"Of course, it's okay," Father Alan said, settling back into his chair.

Bethany hurried to the bedroom where she kept her purse and pulled out the box. She paused with it in her hands, part of her wanting to hold on to the mystery, the other part knowing she had waited long enough. It was time to find out what was inside.

She was met by three curious expressions when she returned to the table and sat the box down in front of her. "This gift is what set me on my journey to meeting all of you, so it only seems appropriate I should open it in your presence. Before my mother passed away, she made me promise I would return it to Nicholas Smith by Christmas Eve. The only information she left me with was his name and address. Since Nicholas is no longer with us and

Christopher said he didn't want it, I'm hoping you'll know what I should do with it."

Mrs. Snyder laid her hand on top of Bethany's. "Go ahead, Bethany. You know we'll help you anyway we can."

Bethany removed the gold wrapping from around the box and took in a deep breath. Lifting off the top revealed nothing at first but a layer of soft, white stuffing. She glanced at the eyes watching closely as her fingers took away the stuffing to reveal what was underneath. It wasn't until she took hold of the ribbon and pulled it out that she heard the sound. She wiggled it back and forth to hear it again while her eyes remained fixed on the object. It was a shiny brass sleigh bell. When Bethany looked up again, there wasn't a mouth that wasn't open.

"Well, I'll be," Joe said. "That looks like one of Nicholas's bells. His initials should be imprinted on it if it is."

Bethany wanted to keep ringing it, but she stopped to search for an *NS*. "It does, I see them right at the top." Her voice lifted with her smile as she continued staring at the bell. "But there's something else...a number."

She handed the bell to Joe to be passed around. "What do you think it means?"

Father Alan rubbed his chin. "I once heard that Nicholas would make a special bell each year to give to someone on Christmas Eve, someone he felt needed to find hope again. I've never known anyone who received one, however, or they've kept it a secret."

Bethany's mind began to spin. "That is a wonderful story, but it doesn't make any sense. Why would my mother have been in Snow Valley on a Christmas Eve and why would Nicholas think she needed this bell? If the number is the year it was given to her, I wouldn't have been more than a few weeks old."

Mrs. Snyder was still cradling the bell that had been passed to her. "If you don't mind me asking, Bethany, what was your mother's name?"

"It was Miriam," Bethany answered.

If she thought she had seen Mrs. Snyder's face turn pale earlier, it was in no way as pale as it was at that very moment.

Chapter Eighteen

Despite Mrs. Snyder's claim that nothing was wrong, Bethany insisted Mrs. Snyder go on to bed while Joe took Father Alan home and she finished cleaning up the kitchen. Though she followed to bed soon afterward, Bethany had a difficult time falling asleep. She couldn't stop worrying about Mrs. Snyder, hoping she wasn't coming down with something. That was twice in one day she hadn't looked well. If Mrs. Snyder hadn't been sitting down both times, Bethany feared she may have fainted.

Besides her concern for Mrs. Snyder, keeping her awake, however, was the uniqueness of the bell. Her eyes kept admiring the petal-like design surrounding the opening, but mostly she didn't want to stop ringing it. She could almost hear the hope in its sound and imagined that several of them together could produce joy from even the grumpiest heart.

She studied the number again and shook her head. Her mother had to have been in Snow Valley, or how else would she have met Nicholas. But why would she have been there with an almost newborn baby? While Bethany was glad to have opened the box, finding out what was inside had only created more questions, ones she wasn't sure she would ever know the answers to.

Bethany picked up the sketchpad and pencils Joe had brought her and flipped back the cover. With Nell's inspiration, Bethany began sketching ideas for a new purse line until she could no longer keep her eyes from closing. By the time she opened them again, she smelled fresh coffee brewing. That was a hopeful indicator Mrs. Snyder was up and feeling better.

Bethany put on her robe and went into the kitchen, but no one was in there. She went ahead and took a cup from the cabinet as Mrs. Snyder walked in, looking like she had just woken up.

"I'm glad to see Joe made the coffee before he left. I didn't plan to sleep in so long this morning," she said.

"Sit down and I'll serve you some," Bethany offered while grabbing another cup.

Bethany watched Mrs. Snyder pull out a chair from the table, moving slower than she usually did. She set the cups on the table and sat down beside her. "Are you feeling better today?"

Mrs. Snyder briefly closed her eyes as she nodded, a soft smile forming when she reopened them and looked at Bethany.

"And you're certain you don't need to see a doctor?" Bethany continued questioning.

"I'm certain," Mrs. Snyder answered with her eyes still on Bethany. "I'll be fine."

Bethany wasn't at all convinced and was determined to keep a close eye on her, especially while they were decorating the church. "As long as you promise, I think I'll try to catch Christopher at the café this morning before the hanging of the greens. Maybe if he sees the bell, he'll change his mind about wanting it."

"I promise, but considering his sour disposition, do you still believe he should have it?" Mrs. Snyder's raised eyebrows punctuated her question.

Bethany took in a thoughtful breath. "I get the feeling, it's for that reason, that he should. Somehow, I think he needs it. And besides, if the bell was meant for me, my mother wouldn't have made me promise to return it."

"The bells do seem to have a way about them." The corners of Mrs. Snyder's mouth lifted briefly. "I plan to leave soon to work in the clothes closet for a while first. There are some new donations and items that have been returned."

"It was just a thought to meet Christopher today. Why don't I help you instead?" Bethany suggested.

"No, you go ahead. It won't take me long," Mrs. Snyder was quick to answer as she reached to squeeze Bethany's hand before standing back up. "I'm going to get dressed now. I'll see you at the church in a little bit."

Bethany did the same and walked into The Daily Bread a few minutes before 8:00. She picked a table to wait from, where she wouldn't miss seeing Christopher come in, yet wouldn't be immediately noticed.

Charlene soon bustled over to set a mug down in front of her and begin pouring coffee. "Looks like you made it just in time, darlin'," she said through her smile.

Bethany followed the path of Charlene's eyes to see Christopher open the door and head toward an empty stool at the counter. He didn't so much as even glance in her direction as he sat down.

With his back toward her, Bethany had a better opportunity to observe him while she watched Charlene take his order. While she wasn't purposefully listening in, she couldn't help but overhear his request for two eggs, sunny side up with a short stack of pancakes. It was the most pleasant she had ever heard him speak.

Christopher must have sensed someone looking at him because as soon as Charlene walked off, he turned far enough around for their eyes to meet.

"You're late, you know," Bethany said with a bit of a wry grin.

He frowned, obviously puzzled. "I don't recall making plans to meet again."

"We didn't," Bethany answered matter-of-factly. "I was just informed you would be here at 8:00 and that's the time you walked in. Have you never heard the saying, 'If you're early, you're on time; If you're on time, you're late'?"

Christopher's face relaxed enough to mirror Bethany's grin. "The saying doesn't count if you made plans without my knowledge."

Bethany gave him an innocent shrug. "Would you care to join me?"

Christopher hesitated before he moved from the stool to her table and sat in the chair across from her. Bethany caught Charlene's wink as he did.

She then looked him in the eye and shook her head. "I don't know that I've ever met anyone quite like you."

Christopher actually smiled without taking his eyes off of her. "I know for certain I haven't met anyone like you. First, I arrive in Snow Valley during a historic snowstorm, and then I meet you and haven't had a moment of peace since."

Charlene brought Christopher's breakfast and placed it down in front of him. "Can I get you anything Bethany?"

Bethany's eyes drifted over to a glass covered stand on the counter. "How about one of those luscious looking cinnamon rolls?"

"You won't be sorry," she said, writing the order on a ticket. "I'll warm it up for you."

There was a short period of silence as Bethany's mind wrestled with what to say next. There were so many things she wanted to know about Christopher and his father, she didn't know where to start. She was also a little apprehensive and decided to wait until he had finished salting and peppering his eggs, seeing that Charlene was also on her way back with her roll.

"How's your breakfast? If it's anything like this cinnamon roll, I'd eat here every morning if I could," Bethany eventually said, following a couple of bites.

"And that's why I'm here every morning when I'm in Snow Valley," he responded.

"Sounds like you'll miss The Daily Bread after you sell the place," she prodded a bit further.

Christopher's head tilted when he looked at her again. "If you think that's enough to change my mind, it won't. I've already made my decision."

Bethany lifted her shoulders. "Just wouldn't want you to hurry into something you might regret. I heard your father was quite a bell maker. I'd love to see where he made them."

This time Christopher looked confused. "That's a part of the past now, and why would you care anyway?"

Bethany leaned in over the table to answer. "Because it's a part of my past, too."

The muscles in Christopher's jaw stiffened. "Whatever it is you're looking for, I can't help you," he said, pulling money from his billfold to cover his meal.

She anticipated she might touch a nerve. "Please, all I'm looking for is some answers. Could you at least confirm that your father made a special bell each year to give someone on Christmas Eve?"

Christopher had already stood up when he acquiesced. "I've heard about it, but he never revealed who he gave one to, so I couldn't tell you for sure. Sorry, I'm moving on with my life."

Bethany's fingers were grasping the bell in her pocket when he turned to leave. Knowing this may be her last chance, she pulled it out and rang it. Christopher had only taken a few steps when he jerked to a sudden stop and whipped around, staring at the bell, and then her.

Their gazes locked while Bethany felt the entire café, holding its breath. "I opened the gift."

Chapter Nineteen

Bethany put the bell back into her coat pocket as she watched Christopher return to the table.

"Where did you get that?" he asked as if he didn't quite believe what he had just seen and heard.

"It's the gift I promised my mother I'd return to your father by Christmas Eve. Since that was no longer possible, I then tried to give it to you. When you refused to take the gift, I opened it myself," she answered.

"I had no idea what the gift was," Christopher attempted to defend himself.

"That's because it was a *gift*. You know those packages you usually have to unwrap before you know what's inside," Bethany smugly joked.

One side of Christopher's mouth slipped into a partial smile. "I suppose I deserved that. May I hold it?"

Bethany eyed him while taking her time to answer. "I'll make you a deal. You show me where your father made his bells, and it's yours to keep. I'm helping with the hanging of the greens at the church this morning, but I'm free after that. I don't mind coming by."

Christopher hesitated, seeming to calculate her offer. "You have a deal."

"Great, I'll see you this afternoon then." Bethany was careful not to come across as gloating over her small victory. She had managed to pry apart his defenses a little further, but knew it wouldn't take much for him to seal them right back up.

As soon as Christopher left the café, Charlene dropped herself into the chair he no longer occupied. "I was in the kitchen, but I could have sworn I heard a bell ring."

Bethany nodded. "You did. It's one Nicholas gave my mother that I'm now giving to Christopher. Would you like to see it?"

"I would love to," she answered, her eyes growing wide as Bethany took it from her pocket and handed it to her.

Bethany watched with piqued interest as Charlene turned it with her fingers and shook her head.

"There's no question Nicholas made this. I didn't even need to see his initials," she said, looking up. "Your mother was a fortunate woman to have one, as rare as these are."

"From what I understand, even rarer because it has the year engraved on it as well, in case you missed seeing it," Bethany said.

Charlene's eyes flew back to the top of the bell, producing a small gasp. "Why, it's the year Nell was born."

"And me," Bethany added with a smile.

A look of bewilderment crossed Charlene's face as she returned the bell to Bethany in slow motion. "I don't know what's taking place here, but I'm beginning to think it's nothing short of a small miracle."

Her words stayed suspended in the air until she abruptly waved her arm and chuckled. "Because that's the longest I've ever seen Christopher sit at a table with someone in quite a while."

"I suppose I should be flattered," Bethany followed with her own chuckle. "But it doesn't make sense why he seems so hardened and distant. This town's nickname is Smithville, after his ancestors, and by all accounts, his mother and father were beloved by everyone."

Charlene got up from the table to remove the dirty plates. "The rumor is guilt, but you didn't hear it from me. She gave Bethany one more bewildered glance then shook her head. "We'll see you later, hon."

Bethany remained seated, thinking back on what she had heard about Christopher during the time she had been in Snow Valley. Father Alan first mentioned the difficult time he had after his mother died. Then Joe said he had spent years trying to make up for being late. The guilt must be connected to whatever he was late for.

She looked at the clock on the wall to check the time. It was too early to arrive at the church for the hanging of the greens, but maybe she could help out Mrs. Snyder for a bit beforehand. Bethany buttoned her coat and left the café to start walking toward St. Paul's, happily accompanied by the occasional jingle in her pocket.

With thirty minutes to spare, Bethany decided to check for Mrs. Snyder in the clothes closet first. She noticed the door was ajar as soon as she descended the stairway. "I'm here to help," she announced, turning through the doorway.

Mrs. Snyder closed the registry as she did. "I must have not heard you coming."

"I'm sorry, I'll warn you better next time," Bethany laughed, relieved to see her looking more like her normal self. "Are you already finished with the new donations?"

"I just finished recording them and sorting them on the table. All I have left is to check the pockets," she answered.

"I never thought about checking pockets," Bethany remarked, walking over to the table.

Mrs. Snyder smiled. "I've found jewelry and keys among other assorted items in them, I'm sure weren't intended to be donated. I keep them in a special box in my office in case the owners ever come looking for them."

Bethany removed her coat and began to go through a stack of adult size clothing first, while Mrs. Snyder started on the children's, searching every piece that had pockets. So far, she had only found a single glove and what looked to be a slip of paper from a fortune cookie. "Today is your lucky day," she said aloud.

"It always is," Mrs. Snyder said with a wink. "Which reminds me, did you have any luck with Christopher this morning at The Daily Bread?"

Bethany grabbed some hangers before answering. "A little. He wanted to hold the bell, but I made a deal with him instead. I told him he could keep it if he showed me where Nicholas made them. Since he agreed, I'm going there this afternoon, hoping I'll discover something that might explain why my mother had the bell. That would be the best luck I could have today."

"Then that is what I'll wish for you." Mrs. Snyder then glanced at her watch. "It's almost 10:00. Why don't you go ahead and let Doris and Kathryn know I'll be right there? I happen to know the whole upstairs smells like Christmas, between the greens and the wassail."

"Sounds wonderful, but I hate to leave you with work left to do."

"I only have a few returns to check in. Don't worry, you'll have plenty of work to do as soon as Doris sets her sights on you. She's especially excited to have your help this year."

Bethany grabbed her coat and purse and headed up the stairs, breathing in the scents of the season that grew stronger with each step. How could decorating ever be considered work?

Chapter Twenty

Two hours passed quickly with Doris and Kathryn in charge, directing where and how the greens were to be hung. Large wreaths with red bows were hung on the outside doors while smaller ones adorned the ends of each pew. The garlands were then draped along railings and doorways, while smaller sprigs of greens were placed around the candles in the windows and the table displaying the nativity scene. Last, were the poinsettias to be arranged on either side of the altar.

Bethany stood at the back of the church, admiring all they had accomplished. The decorations added the simple, but perfect touch for celebrating the holiday. She hadn't expected to feel as worn out as she did, but she wasn't about to allow any of the other ladies to take her place on the ladder, especially Mrs. Snyder. Never mind the argument that they had been doing it for years. She lifted her fingers to her nose another time, not wanting to wash away the scent the needles had left behind, but it was time for lunch.

The meal consisting of ham and turkey sandwiches and lively conversation, topped the morning off. Bethany listened closely to this group of women that had welcomed her into their circle with open arms. It hadn't taken long to see how dedicated they were to the church, the community, and each other.

"Do you need me to take you back to the house to get your car?" Mrs. Snyder asked once they were done eating.

"I don't mind walking, since I know you have some work to finish up in the office. The fresh air will do me some good," she answered. "I'll see you back home."

Mrs. Snyder gave her a thoughtful smile. "At home then, but be careful."

Bethany said the rest of her good-byes and set out on her walk. For some reason she couldn't stop humming, one Christmas song after another, hesitating only when "Let It Snow" came to mind. Bethany grinned and hummed it anyway. A little more snow might actually be welcome, now that she was staying in Snow Valley for the holidays.

Since she would be passing Joe's store on her way, Bethany decided to stop in for a quick hello. She was reaching for the door when it opened in front of her.

Nell laughed at Bethany's surprise. "I was just on my way out."

"I'm glad I ran into you," Bethany said. "I was wanting to come by your shop tomorrow afternoon. Would 1:00 be all right?"

"That would be great, but we should make it 2:00, in case the café gets extra busy," Nell suggested then hesitated. "The shop isn't much to see, Bethany, but I'm happy to show it to you."

Bethany smiled. "Nell, I've seen what comes out of your shop, and that's all I care about."

Nell returned the smile. "Till tomorrow then."

Bethany entered the store and walked up to the register where Joe was reorganizing the shelves behind it. "I'd offer to help you, but my arms are worn out from this morning."

Joe tossed his head back with a knowing chuckle. "The hanging of the greens isn't for the weak, is it?"

"No, but it was fun, and next time I'll make sure I'm in better shape. I mean, if there is a next time, or at least I hope there is," she answered, stumbling through her words.

"You know nothing would make Mrs. Snyder and me happier than for you to come to Snow Valley and stay with us anytime, but especially at Christmas," Joe said.

The mention of Mrs. Snyder's name reminded Bethany of the main reason she had stopped in. "I tried to keep an eye on her today, making sure she wasn't working too hard, but that wasn't near as easy as I thought it would be."

This time Joe released a full-bellied laugh. "Now you can understand how hard my job has been these past few decades."

Bethany took a moment to enjoy the laughter with him. "In all seriousness, though, I've been a little worried about her," she gently pressed.

His expression became more subdued. "This is Mrs. Snyder's favorite time of year, and I think she tends to overdue, is all."

She did her best to believe him. "I guess I should be off to Christopher's now. I told him I'd come by this afternoon."

Joe put his hand to his chin. "Hmm...I thought he was acting kind of funny when he dropped by this morning."

"Funny, in a good way?" Her eye's widened with the question.

His hand remained on his chin to answer. "Let's just say, not in a bad way."

Bethany couldn't help but be curious by Joe's comment and was glad she had a few more blocks to gather her thoughts before getting in her car and driving out to see him again. To be honest, she didn't really want to give the bell away anymore, but it was part of the promise and now, it was part of the deal.

Turning down Oaktree Lane gave Bethany pause. It truly was a picturesque scene of snow-covered trees, with peeks of the valley tucked in between. She imagined it would be an inspiring view for any type of workshop.

Christopher opened the front door before she had even knocked. "Come in."

Bethany tried not to show her surprise as she did. The dusty pieces of furniture she expected to see, were actually high polished antiques of intricate design, reflecting light from both the lamps and the fireplace. The look was authentic and inviting.

"This is a very cozy home," she remarked, continuing to gaze around the room. Her eyes stopped when she saw the pictures on the mantle, and she walked over to take a closer look. There was one of a man holding a leather strap of sleigh bells that she knew must be Nicholas. She glanced at Christopher, and then back. Even with the man's beard, their features were too similar not to be father and son.

"That's my father with the first set of bells he ever completed," Christopher said.

Bethany acknowledged the information with a nod while her eyes shifted to the picture next to it. Nicholas had his arms around a woman on one side and a young boy on the other.

"I'm sure you can figure out that's my mother and me," he added. "It's the last picture taken of the three of us before she died."

"Amelie," Bethany said in a whispered voice, her eyes lingering on the picture a little longer.

"It's pretty cold in the shed. May I get you something hot to drink?" Christopher asked.

Bethany turned to look at him, a bit amused by his new role as host. "What do you have?"

"I made some hot mochas, if you like them."

"Coffee and chocolate, what's not to like?"

Christopher left for the kitchen and returned with two mugs. "Are you ready to see where the bells were made?"

Bethany took one of the mugs he extended toward her and followed him outside to the shed that was his father's workshop. She could tell Christopher had tried to warm it with a couple of portable heaters, but it was more than just pretty cold inside.

"How did he work in here," she asked.

"When you're melting brass at 1600 degrees, it does warm up a lot faster," he answered, one corner of his mouth, lifting into half a smile.

Christopher continued, showing her the cauldron used for melting the brass, along with the sand packed molds and the tumbler for polishing. He even showed her the bells he had attempted to make himself.

"Why aren't you still making them?" she said, picking up one of the bells and looking at him more directly.

Christopher shrugged. "I can't seem to get them to turn out like my father's."

Bethany tipped her head. "So, that's why you're selling the place. You're giving up."

"I'm not giving up. I just don't think it's worth wasting any more of my time on," he said, looking away as if he were needing to convince himself as much as Bethany.

Bethany reached in her pocket, pulled out the bell, and rang it. "You don't think this is worth it?"

Christopher's eyes quickly returned to the bell.

"You kept your portion of the deal, and I'm keeping mine. Here," she said holding it out for him to take. "It's yours."

He lifted the bell from Bethany's hand and began examining it. "My father wanted me to learn how to make bells like this for years. I helped out some when it was convenient, but I had more important pursuits to follow, first hockey, then college. The weekend I finally promised to come home for him to teach me, I was invited to the biggest hockey game of the season. He told me not to worry, to come home the next weekend. Only there never was a next weekend. I was too late."

Bethany now understood what Father Alan and Charlotte's words had meant, and the terrible weight he carried for having broken a promise. "And you've been trying to teach yourself ever since. From what I can see, you've almost mastered them," she encouraged him.

Christopher was still examining the bell. "I'm missing something though. The question is what?"

Bethany's heart was filled with sympathy, witnessing his struggle. "I wish I had the answer for you." She picked up her purse and took out her keys. "I should go now, but thank you for the hot mocha and showing me your father's workshop."

He looked back up at her, his face revealing a greater sense of peace. "I was afraid I would never hold one of these again. Thank you."

"You're welcome." Bethany paused as she started to leave. "I'm sorry you were too late to see your father again, but maybe, in a way yet to be revealed, you've been right on time. You said it took hours of tumbling in harsh elements to smooth out the rough edges of the bell and make it beautiful. I'm not so sure we're any different."

She closed the door behind her and hurried to her car, suddenly feeling light headed. Bethany could only hope, that despite what Joe said, she and Mrs. Snyder weren't both coming down with something. Once in the driver's seat, she took a couple of breaths before starting the engine. There was no doubt she had been doing a lot of thinking lately, though Bethany realized it hadn't been about her job with Touché, or even more surprising, Kenneth.

Chapter Twenty-one

Bethany drove back to the Snyder's, not knowing any more about why Nicholas gave her mother the bell than she did before. She hadn't wanted to ask Christopher too many questions, using her eyes instead to search for clues inside the workshop for something Nicholas might have recorded the bells in. Bethany was sure he would have at least kept track of the ones he had sold and to whom.

There were three days left until Christmas, three days left to find the missing pieces to her personal puzzle. After that, who knew if she would ever see Christopher again, especially if he did sell the property. What was there would most likely be discarded, sold, or given away. Bethany doubted there was much Christopher would keep for himself. She would have to figure out a way to go back and look again. And soon.

The chime of a new text, surprised Bethany as she pulled up in front of the house. Seeing it was from Kenneth made her wish she hadn't looked.

How's it going?

She hesitated to respond, not knowing how upset he still was over their vacation. *It's going okay.*

Remaining tentative she added, *I'm sorry our plans got messed up.*

I'm sorry, too. Did you ever find out what was inside the gift that was so important?

Her thumbs typed an answer, hovering over the keyboard before she inhaled slowly and pushed send. *It was a hand cast sleigh bell.*

She held her breath, expecting words of scolding disapproval to spew onto her screen. They never did, but it didn't take seeing them for her to know what they would have said. If there had been any chance of saving her relationship with Kenneth before, Bethany was sure it was gone now. He would never accept that a single sleigh bell was important enough to miss a vacation over, even though the snowstorm itself wasn't her fault.

Bethany got out of her car and saw the front door open with Mrs. Snyder standing in its space. She hurried up the sidewalk and into the house to get them both out of the cold.

"I saw you pull up and was beginning to think you were never going to come inside," Mrs. Snyder said as she closed the door behind her. "Did everything go okay with Christopher?"

Bethany smiled as she pulled off her scarf and unbuttoned her coat. "It went fine. I loved seeing the workshop and learning how the bells are made. Christopher even let me see the ones he's made himself. They may not be quite like his father's but they're still special."

Mrs. Snyder nodded in thought. "Hmm…that means he's come to trust you."

"I don't know why he wouldn't. I don't bite," Bethany giggled."

"I don't think it's that easy for Christopher. He hasn't let many people into his life since both his parents have been gone."

"I wonder why."

"Some people sadly believe it's better to pretend you don't have a heart than to have it hurt again. Add to it, that you have a lot of similar traits as Amelie, smart, pretty and confident with a big heart, and I think that scares him."

Bethany released a sigh. "I may act confident, but I'm just a small-town girl who grew up in a small house with her mother and little else. The truth is, no matter how hard I try to prove myself, I never quite feel deserving of anything that comes my way, including Kenneth."

Mrs. Snyder threw her a look of admonishment. "Bethany Mason, you are loved just the way you are. You don't have to prove anything to anyone…most of all, Kenneth."

"Thank you, Mrs. Snyder." Bethany managed a smile while she paused to release a breath. "Speaking of Kenneth, he just texted me. That's why it took me a little longer to get out of the car."

Anticipation widened Mrs. Snyder's eyes. "And?"

"He knows the gift I was returning for my mother, was a sleigh bell," she answered, then pressed her lips together.

Mrs. Snyder's gaze held fast to Bethany's. "I gather he wasn't impressed," she concluded.

Bethany shook her head. "At least I assume he wasn't. He quit texting after I told him."

"It might help to call him and try to explain," Mrs. Snyder suggested.

"It might, but I'll wait until after Christmas. I doubt it would make any difference before then, and I just want to enjoy my time in Snow Valley," she answered.

Mrs. Snyder smiled. "I happened to be vacuuming this afternoon and noticed your sketchpad left open on the nightstand. That's a lovely purse design you drew. I bet there are more, aren't there?"

Bethany gave her a sheepish nod.

"Have you ever thought about showing them to your company? I can't imagine they wouldn't like your ideas," Mrs. Snyder continued.

"I did once. They liked them well enough, but Touché has a brand image to maintain that my designs don't fit into," she explained. "I quit designing after that, until I came here and saw Nell's work. Her skills inspired me all over again."

Mrs. Snyder's face brightened. "I thought I detected a bit of Nell in the extra touches. How about starting your own purse line together?"

Bethany grinned. "I can't deny it would be a dream come true, but it's not that easy."

"There's not much worthwhile that is. But if anyone can do it, I believe you can. You're full of good ideas, Bethany, like selling some of the vintage pieces from the clothes closet to provide extra funds for the church."

"I should probably keep some ideas to myself. You already have enough work to do at the church."

"Well, I'm glad you didn't. Father Alan and I have already discussed implementing the plan next year with a goal of expanding the closet.

"Then put me down as your first customer. I can't wait to buy the coat."

"Of course," Mrs. Snyder said, then shook her head. "I can't imagine seeing it on anyone else."

With a spark of new inspiration, Bethany retrieved her sketchpad and spent the rest of the day, before and after dinner, continuing to draw out more ideas. It couldn't have been a more peaceful evening, hearing the occasional pop of embers from the fireplace and the soothing sounds of Christmas coming from the stereo, all while Mrs. Snyder was beside her and Joe was in the chair straight across, reading.

It wasn't much longer until Joe closed his book and stood up. "I think it's time I get a head start on some extra rest, being on standby for Santa you know. With talk of more snow coming by Christmas, he may need my help," he added with a wink.

His words prompted Bethany to follow suit with her sketchpad. "I hope you're not teasing about the snow, Joe."

Joe chuckled. "I figured you'd had enough snow by now."

"Christmas snow is different." Bethany smiled as she leaned over to give Mrs. Snyder a quick hug. "I'll see you in the morning."

Finished getting ready for bed, Bethany slipped under the covers and turned off the lamp beside her. She pulled the blanket and quilt up underneath her chin, but it was more than their comfort keeping her warm. Maybe it was the unrestrained laughter that accompanied the sandwiches after the hanging of the greens, or the memory of the hot mocha Christopher had made for her…maybe it was the luster of gold hues in his hazel eyes that seemed to match the bell's, or the sharing of her purse designs with Mrs. Snyder in front of the Christmas tree. Maybe it was all of it. Maybe it was just the unspoken magic of this place.

She smiled as she could almost hear Mrs. Snyder's words again, *Bethany Mason, you are loved just the way you are...* There was no doubt, Bethany did feel loved in Snow Valley. What was suddenly intriguing, however, was that she couldn't recall ever mentioning her last name.

Chapter Twenty-two

Bethany was glad to see Mrs. Snyder already up the next morning, seemingly well-rested and humming in the kitchen. The song was none other than "Jingle Bells."

"Oh, to someday be able to go dashing through the snow in an open sleigh," Bethany said with a sigh as she walked in to join her.

Mrs. Snyder's face was beaming when she looked at Bethany to respond. "How about if that someday is tomorrow?"

Bethany's mouth dropped in disbelief. "A real sleighride?"

"As real as they come," Mrs. Snyder answered, grinning broadly. "There's a farm just outside of town that does special rides this time of year, as long as there's been enough snow."

"I wonder if it's the same farm Father Alan told me about," Bethany said, thinking of Nicholas's bells as well.

"I'm sure it is. Winterhaven Farm has been around for at least a hundred years, and it seems almost that long since I've been," she reminisced. "I've already let them know we're coming and Joe has already asked Joe Jr. to mind the store."

Bethany clasped her hands together as her heels bounced off the floor in anticipation. "I don't know how I'm supposed to wait until tomorrow."

It was then that an abrupt thought took her by surprise, causing her to look questioningly at Mrs. Snyder. "Would you mind if I invited someone to go with us?"

"Not at all," Mrs. Snyder answered. "Are you thinking of Nell since you'll be seeing her this afternoon?"

Bethany bit her lip and shook her head. "I was thinking of Christopher, but it's okay if you'd rather I didn't."

Mrs. Snyder's mouth twisted into a smile while giving an affirming nod. "It would be very nice of you to invite Christopher. Our ride is scheduled for 11:00."

"I also wanted to ask him if I could look around the workshop another time as well, mostly so I can take some pictures to help me remember it better. Though, I do still hope the answers I'm needing are somewhere inside the house or workshop," Bethany said.

Mrs. Snyder glanced at the clock on the wall. "If you hurry, you should be able to catch him at the cafe."

Bethany figured she had approximately thirty minutes to get there before Christopher finished his last bite of breakfast. Normally, she would choose to walk the short distance, but driving would get her there faster, and she'd already have a car in case he agreed to let her see the workshop again.

"It's worth a try," she said, practically running back to her room to get dressed. While she had picked out a few more items to borrow from the closet, her options for what to wear each day were limited. At least she couldn't use up all her time, deciding. She threw on the only sweater she hadn't worn yet along with the flannel-lined jeans she had been wearing every day. A smirk crossed her face at the thought of how horrified Kenneth would be to see her in these clothes.

Grabbing her coat and purse, Bethany started toward the door to leave. "Wish me luck. I'll come by the church sometime before I meet Nell at 2:00."

"Okay." Mrs. Snyder smiled. "You know you can always count on my best wishes."

The words accompanied Bethany to her car, settling in her thoughts while she started the engine. With a boost of confidence, she headed for the café. It was only a few minutes after 8:00. Surely Christopher was still eating or drinking his coffee.

The café seemed very busy inside when she pulled into a parking space. Her eyes searched for the black sedan she had seen at his house the day before, but it was nowhere in sight. It could be he had to park farther away.

Bethany reminded herself of Mrs. Snyder's wishes and walked inside. Her eyes scanned the barstools at the counter, first, where Christopher was most likely to be. She hadn't considered that he might be with someone, until she didn't see him perched on top of any of them. It was then that she resorted to searching the tables, stopping at one against the wall. Christopher was with someone all right, a woman with perfectly styled blonde hair, wearing a cream wool blazer, who didn't at all appear to be from Snow Valley. Bethany felt a rush of heat spill across her cheeks, but couldn't spin around fast enough before he saw her.

She gave him a quick wave, wanting only to get out of there as quickly as possible and spare herself any more humiliation. Somehow, she would have to pretend that he wasn't the reason she was there or that she had to leave because there was no place for her to sit. But as if the thought alone possessed enough power to boot a man off a barstool, one stood up and walked away. Bethany had no choice but to proceed in that direction and claim it, especially since Charlene's arm was firmly prompting her to do so.

"Glad to see you this morning. I heard you're meeting up with Nell this afternoon," Charlene said, starting to pour Bethany a cup of coffee.

Bethany could see that Charlene's eyes were glued elsewhere and put her hand out to stop her before there was a spilled mess on the counter. "Thanks, Charlene, that's enough for now. You sure are busy today."

"That's a good thing, but if there's something special you want to order, you better do it now before I run out," she commented, though her eyes were still distracted.

"Are you okay, Charlene?" Bethany asked with both curiosity and concern in her voice.

Charlene jerked her attention away long enough to answer. "I'm just watching a fish swim around its bait. Word is she's a potential buyer for the Smith place, though what she would want with it, I don't have a clue."

That was all Bethany needed to hear to know Charlene was talking about Christopher and his guest. It was a sad reminder there would soon be no more Smiths in a town nicknamed Smithville. "Are you sure she's the fish and he's the bait?"

Charlene chuckled. "Can't say I am, but I have a pretty good hunch. Now, what is it I can get for you?"

Bethany hadn't planned to order breakfast, but she was hungry so she may as well stay and eat. "How about an egg and sausage this morning?"

"Coming right up," she said, giving the table one more glance before rushing off.

Like Charlene, Bethany found it interesting why this woman would want to purchase the Smith property. It was serenely tucked away, but that was just it. Right or wrong, if she were going by first impressions, this woman didn't look the type to want to live in a charming, yet simple, old and secluded home in the woods. If only she had the money, Bethany pondered, she would buy the property herself.

Charlene brought her food and walked away, then returned again, almost as quickly. Bethany expected the reason was to refill her coffee, but Charlene set something down beside her plate instead, before continuing on. Bethany looked to see it was one of the café's paper napkins that had been folded in half. There were napkin dispensers on every table and along the entire counter. She wasn't sure why Charlene had made a specific effort to give her one.

Bethany finished her last couple of bites and laid her fork on her plate before picking up the napkin to unfold it. That's when she realized it hadn't been meant for her to use, but to read. *How about sharing a table?* was handwritten inside.

She couldn't imagine who would have asked Charlene to deliver the question, but her head only had to turn a few degrees around to find out. The woman who had been sitting with Christopher was no longer there. Her eyes met his as he extended his hand toward the, now, empty chair.

Bethany placed some money on her ticket, grabbed her coffee cup, and slid off the barstool. In a few steps, she had taken the other woman's place.

Christopher's mouth slipped into a smile. "I'm guessing this means yes."

Chapter Twenty-three

"Well, I do feel a certain obligation to set the record straight. Is she a girlfriend, or as word would have it, someone interested in buying your property?"

Christopher grunted lightly. "I'd forgotten how quickly news passes from lips to ears around here."

Bethany continued to look at him with further expectation. "That's not an answer, you know."

"How about definitely not, and possibly. In that exact order," he clarified.

"Still not good enough if you want to keep the rumors at bay," she insisted.

"Maybe I'm okay with rumors," Christopher countered.

Bethany rolled her eyes and sighed, knowing Christopher was now jesting.

"Kate is a real estate associate of mine who is always scouting properties for sale. That's really all there is to tell."

"While your property is lovely, I'm not sure someone like Kate would be happy, living in a town like Snow Valley."

Christopher's head tilted in thought. "Kate wouldn't be the one living here. She's not interested in properties for herself, only in negotiating for other investors and developers. It was awfully nice of you to consider her happiness, however."

Bethany glanced out the window to take her next breath. Of course, she wanted everyone to be happy, but her real reason for the comment was to help sway Christopher from selling.

"What about you? Would you be happy in a place like Snow Valley?" he asked, sweeping her attention back to him.

She looked into his face, deciding how to answer.

"It's only fair, I get to ask you a question," Christopher continued.

Bethany crossed her arms and leaned on the table. "I'll answer any question you ask me on one condition."

Christopher laughed. "I should have known there would be another deal."

"All you have to do is show me your father's workshop again."

"But I've already shown you once. There's nothing else to see."

"Maybe not for you, but I think there still might be something there for me. The sooner we go, the sooner I'll answer your questions," she reminded him.

Christopher rubbed his chin. "What kind of work is it you do for a living?"

Bethany pressed her lips together and shrugged.

"All right, I give," Christopher said, lifting his hands in surrender. "Looks like we're headed to the workshop."

Bethany stood up from the table, waved to Charlene and led the way out the door. "Where are you parked?"

Christopher pointed to the old pickup in front of them. "Right here. It could use some new paint, but, surprisingly, it still shifts as smooth as it ever did."

Bethany smiled. It was no wonder she hadn't seen his car. "I'll follow you there."

She let him back out of his parking spot first and was soon driving behind him down Main Street and onto Oaktree Lane. Without a doubt he had become more relaxed and less defensive around her. Bethany couldn't help but think it was Snow Valley working its palpable magic on him. Whatever it was, she was thankful he cared enough about her answering a few questions to accept another deal.

Pulling up in front of the house, Bethany watched Christopher as he got out of the pickup. He didn't seem near as out of place on the property as when she first visited him. It had taken a few days, but something told her he was never happier than when he came home, even if he didn't show it. By the time the layers of his persona in the city were stripped away, it was time to put them on again. She got the impression he never would have considered selling if he had figured out how to finish the bells as well as his father did.

"It's going to be extra cold inside here since I won't have had time to warm it up," Christopher said while finding the right key to unlock the workshop door.

"I'll be okay," Bethany said, but it didn't take more than a couple of steps through the door, to understand what he meant by extra cold. It was freezing. The portable heaters Christopher began plugging in would take too long to make a difference. "There is something that would warm us up even faster."

Christopher gave her a puzzled look. "Like what?"

"Like letting me watch you make a bell. You did tell me, heating the cauldron to 1600 degrees only took twenty to thirty minutes." Bethany kept her eyes on his while her words lingered. "Think of it as an early Christmas present to me."

His eyes appeared to start twinkling. "That would presume I was going to give you one."

"Well, it is the season of giving, whether it's an actual wrapped present or not. Remember, I tried to give you one of those," she teasingly persisted.

Christopher shook his head, appearing amused. "I suppose it wouldn't hurt anything. Kate won't be getting back with me until later about any potential buyers."

Bethany's eyes grew, surprised he agreed to take her up on making one. She watched him measure the brass into the cauldron and fire up the foundry before walking over to the table. "Can I help with anything?"

"If you want to come over here, I'll teach you how to fill the molds," he offered.

She hurried over to stand the closest she had ever been to him, already feeling warmer.

Christopher turned to look at her, their faces only inches apart. "You can watch how I prepare the bottom half of the mold, and then you can do the same for the top half."

Bethany was glad she only had to nod while an unexpected wave of dizziness passed, a feeling she was quick to blame on too much caffeine. It was easy to lose track of the amount of coffee she was drinking at the cafe, with Charlene constantly topping it off.

Christopher didn't hesitate to start filling the mold with the loose clay. "This is the easiest step before you have to tamp it down like this," he instructed, using a tool to pound the clay out evenly. He then pushed bell halves into the clay to make the imprint. "Now it's your turn."

"I need to take a picture of this first." Bethany didn't give him a chance to refuse, immediately holding up her phone to take several of the mold and Christopher before trading places with him. Sensing his presence right beside her, she did her best to copy what she had just seen him do and smiled when he gave her a look of approval.

"I do believe you're a natural at this," he said. "And since we still have time until the brass finishes melting, you can answer why you wanted to come back to the workshop."

Bethany pressed her lips together. "I guess I do need to honor my part of the deal."

"You did say..." he started.

"I would answer any question." Bethany completed the sentence, then let her eyes scan the inside of the workshop. "Just being in the same place where a master bell maker once worked is part of it. But the real reason is, this is where your father made the special bell he gave my mother, and I don't know why. I don't even know why she was in Snow Valley or how long she stayed or if she ever came back."

Christopher's eyes showed his understanding. "Unless these walls begin to talk, I'm afraid you may never know."

"Didn't he keep records of all the bells he made? Surely there are books or ledgers around here somewhere," Bethany heard herself almost pleading.

"He did keep records, but he never talked about those special bells, so, I doubt they're included." Christopher held his eyes on her while he paused. "I will look to make sure."

"Thank you, that's all I hoped for," she responded with an appreciative smile.

"Now, going back to the question I asked you at the café," Christopher continued. "Do you think you would be happy in a place like Snow Valley?"

Bethany's forehead narrowed. "I don't know if I would have said yes in the beginning of being stranded here, but now, I think I would. I've discovered things I hadn't realized were missing in my life. Who would believe it was a sleigh bell that brought me to Snow Valley? A former boyfriend sure didn't."

"What's his name?"

"Kenneth."

"That's very unlucky for Kenneth then," Christopher said, his eyes locking onto hers.

Bethany turned to escape his gaze before she blushed. "I think it's my turn to ask you something,"

"Okay," he agreed.

Telling herself, the worst he could say was no, she finally blurted out the question. "Would you like to go on a sleigh ride with me and Joe and Mrs. Snyder tomorrow? It's at Winterhaven Farm just outside of town. I mean if—"

"I'd love to go," Christopher interrupted.

She couldn't help her surprise. "Really?"

"Yes, really," he smiled then tipped his head toward the cauldron. "I think our brass should be melted now."

Bethany had a feeling inside of her she couldn't identify. Perhaps it wasn't only the brass that had been melting, perhaps it was all the pretense between them. They were both searching for answers, ones connected to a single, brass sleigh bell.

Chapter Twenty-four

Christopher walked over and carefully removed the cauldron from the foundry to begin pouring the brass into the mold. "As soon as the metal cools, we can separate the mold and pop out the two halves of the bell. Then I can show you how they're put together."

Bethany lowered her phone after taking more pictures and nodded, still feeling the effects of his accepting her invitation to go on the sleighride. "I can't wait."

"You know I didn't agree to a photo shoot," he remarked with half a grin.

"It's a good thing I didn't ask then," she laughed. "I suppose it's because I'm so used to staging shoots for our handbags, and they don't get a choice."

Christopher laughed with her, being prompted then to ask her more questions about her job. Their conversation was easy as she explained what she knew about the handbag industry and its consumers.

"I think the mold has cooled enough now. Shall we find out?" Christopher asked after what seemed like a short period of time.

Bethany could feel her face beaming with a sense of accomplishment. "Yes!"

She watched as he separated the mold and popped out two, almost perfect halves of golden brass, imprinted with the same petal design as the one that had belonged to her mother.

"Next we add the metal ball and braze the two halves together."

Bethany was mesmerized by the skill and patience necessary to complete the process. "May I hold it?"

Christopher handed it to her, in which she wasted no time in shaking to hear its distinct sound.

"The polishing takes the longest amount of time so I'm afraid you won't see it finished today."

"That's okay," she said, handing it back to him. "Maybe I can another time."

Christopher rotated the bell in his fingers. "What time should I meet you out at Winterhaven?"

"Our ride is at 11:00, but we'll come by to pick you up a bit before that," she answered.

Christopher's eyes focused on hers before acknowledging the offer. "Then I'll be ready when you get here."

Bethany glanced at her watch. "I should probably go now. I told Mrs. Snyder I would come by the church before going to Nell's place."

She was finishing buttoning her coat to leave when another word from Christopher made her stop.

"Bethany…"

She looked up and smiled at hearing him say her name out loud for the first time.

"I'm looking forward to tomorrow. Thank you for asking me."

Bethany reached for the doorknob, still smiling. "You're welcome. Consider it my early Christmas present to you."

She heard Christopher chuckle behind her as she stepped outside the door and took a breath of the cold air. Something was different between them, something she dared to wonder was more than just a new friendship.

Bethany drove to the church, hoping to still catch Mrs. Snyder and let her know Christopher would be joining them the next day. She didn't see her car when she pulled up, but Joe might have brought her or she chose to walk, like she often did. As Bethany headed toward the back door leading to the offices, she paused to look across the cemetery. While she never knew any of those who were buried there, it was apparent their love still radiated through the lives they touched.

Once inside the church hallway, Bethany saw that both of the church offices were empty. The doors were open, but the lights were off and no one was in them. She figured they may have stepped out for lunch, but there were a couple of places to check before she left. Bethany heard humming while descending the stairs to the clothes closet. Seeing the light was also on, caused her steps to quicken, having so much she wanted to tell Mrs. Snyder. She turned into the doorway, surprised to see a different figure holding an armful of clothes.

"Father Alan! I didn't expect to find you in here," Bethany said. "Where is Mrs. Snyder?"

"She said she had a few errands to run and asked if I would mind the closet, if necessary," he answered. "Sure enough, we had a young family come in, needing to borrow some warmer clothing. As you can see, I'm still putting away the items that didn't fit."

"Here, let me help." Bethany set her purse down and took off her coat. "In fact, I have some extra time, why don't you just let me finish. That way you can get yourself something to eat."

Father Alan looked hesitant. "I'm sure you could do it much faster, but I hate to leave you by yourself."

Bethany had already started relieving his arms of the clothes. "I'll be fine. Now go, and that's an order."

He chuckled as her hand playfully shooed him out the door. "I imagine Mrs. Snyder will be back soon, but if I see her, I'll let her know you're down here."

Setting the clothes on the small table, Bethany wanted to look through the registry to see if Father Alan had recorded who this family was and which items they had borrowed. At first glance, she didn't see the black book anywhere, but soon found it buried underneath the stack of tried-on jackets.

Bethany opened it up to the last entry. Mrs. Snyder would be pleased Father Alan had remembered to record everything, from their names to each article of clothing they took. Bethany was sure those names would soon be added to Mrs. Snyder's percolator prayers.

It was then that a stronger curiosity took hold and she flipped the pages back to the very beginning. Her eyes scanned the recorded dates and the names next to them until they reached the year she was born, and then slowed down.

Bethany had almost reached the end of that year when she felt the prickly raising of hair on her arms, accompanied by a slight chill.

She dropped into the chair next to her as her head began to spin. Of course, her mother would have had to visit Snow Valley in order to have been given the bell, but there it was in front of her. The evidence was in her mother's own handwriting, *Miriam Mason.*

Tears filled her eyes as a wave of implications came crashing down. Mrs. Snyder had met her mother, and most likely, her as well. She must have looked back on the registry and that was how she knew her last name. But it was the next words she read that completely suspended her breath.

In the column of items borrowed was the description of a coat. Her eyes then shifted to the one she had been wearing. There was no question it was the same coat, making it no longer a coincidence why it fit her so well. She and her mother had always been close in size.

Bethany walked over to where she had taken it off and held it close to her nose. She knew if there had been any remnant of the inexpensive fragrance her mother always wore, it would be long gone by now, but she inhaled deeply, needing to try. As she did, questions began pouring into her mind. *Was her mother wearing this coat when Nicholas gave her the bell?... Did Mrs. Snyder know why her mother was there or where she was going*

"Bethany?" a voice called out, shutting off the flow of contemplation.

Hearing Mrs. Snyder coming down the stairs, Bethany dropped the coat onto the chair and hurriedly closed the registry to put back onto the shelf. She then quickly wiped away any moisture from her eyes that may have still been present.

"Father Alan said you were down here," Mrs. Snyder said as she entered the room. "I'm sorry I was gone when you came."

Bethany calmed her breathing and turned around with a smile, having no intention of letting Mrs. Snyder know what she had found. So many good things had come out of her stay in Snow Valley and she didn't want to risk anything ruining it. The past had already waited this long to reveal itself. It could wait a little longer.

Chapter Twenty-five

Maintaining her smile was more difficult than Bethany expected. One look in Mrs. Snyder's eyes and she had to fight to keep the tears from forming again. She now knew Mrs. Snyder was part of the reason she felt such a strong connection to the town, and because of a special sleigh bell, their paths were crossing again.

Mrs. Snyder's demeanor quickly changed. "Has something upset you, Bethany?"

She shook her head, determined not to give anything away. "I'm just extra happy and excited about tomorrow's sleigh ride. Not only did I get to help Christopher make a bell this morning, when I asked if he would like to join us on the ride, he said yes."

That seemed to be all the explanation necessary for the worry on Mrs. Snyder's face to dissipate. "I'm so glad he's going with us."

"Me, too, though I don't know how I'm going to be able to sit still before then."

If you'd like, I thought we could cut out a large batch of sugar cookies this evening. That should help the time go faster."

"That's a perfect idea! I haven't made cookies like that in so long, I can't even remember," Bethany gushed.

Mrs. Snyder burst into laughter. "I'll go ahead and mix up the dough then as soon as I get home since it needs time to chill. That way we can bake them before dinner and ice them afterward."

Bethany gave her a nod of vigorous approval. "Until then, I thought I'd go on over to Nell's shop and see if she's there. It's a little early, but if she isn't, I can always stop in and say hi to Joe."

Mrs. Snyder gave a sigh. "I think that man is up to something."

It was Bethany's turn to laugh. "Don't worry. It *is* almost Christmas, and I sincerely doubt he could ever do anything that would take him off Santa's nice list."

They had left the room and reached the top of the stairs when Bethany stopped to give Mrs. Snyder a paused look. "Thank you."

"For what?" Mrs. Snyder seemed bewildered.

It took a moment for her to answer. "For everything. I'll see you soon."

With a smile, Bethany continued outside to her car. At that moment, how her mother came to wear this same coat didn't matter near as much as knowing the kindness Mrs. Snyder had shown her, at a time she needed it.

She got into her car and drove the few blocks to Nell's, thankful to see a light on in the shop, indicating she was there. It wasn't that she would have minded seeing Joe, it was just that she was anxious to learn about Nell's work before helping Mrs. Snyder bake cookies. Nell waved to her through the window as she parked. Bethany wasn't sure if this was the right time to show Nell all of her sketches, but she picked up the sketch pad from the passenger's seat, needing to show her at least one of them.

"Hi, Nell," Bethany said as she entered. "I wasn't sure if you had to work the café today, but decide to see if you were here, anyway."

Nell smiled. "It didn't end up being too busy me so I drove out to Winterhaven Farm for a bit."

"We're going there tomorrow for a sleigh ride. Is that why you went?" Bethany asked, excitement returning to her voice.

"Not this time. I wanted to talk to Eliot about a new project I hope to start working on."

"Oh, is Eliot the owner?"

"He's their son," Nell answered, as a light shade of red colored her cheeks.

Bethany smiled as she lifted her chin. "I see."

Nell shook her head. "It's not what you're thinking, Eliot is just a friend."

"One that makes you blush?" Bethany asked still smiling.

"I wasn't blushing," Nell stoically insisted before bursting into giggles. "Though I'm sure I am now."

Bethany giggled along with Nell, watching her face turn even redder. "I promise, I won't tell."

Then letting her eyes begin to wander around the shop, the talent Nell possessed became more obvious. The raw, earthy smell of leather permeated the air as she saw more of Nell's ornaments hanging up along with other pieces of leather displaying a variety of different styles.

"Those are all the samples of the kind of work I can do. They show some of the designs I've made by tooling or embossing and some I've also painted or dyed. Next to those are ones I've appliqued that show some of the different stitches I like to use," Nell explained.

Bethany walked over to take a closer look at each one of them, amazed by all Nell knew how to do. At the end of the samples were straps of leather that looked as if all they were missing were sleigh bells. She pulled off one of the straps to feel it in her hand.

"Nicholas was one of my very first customers. Unfortunately, we didn't get to work together very long before he passed away. Those are some of the straps he never got to use, but I've held on to them just in case I ever need them," Nell said.

"Like, if Christopher were to follow in his father's footsteps," Bethany completed Nell's thought for her.

Nell frowned. "It doesn't look like that's ever going to happen, especially if he sells the property."

"Maybe, but Christmas is a time for miracles," Bethany said, hanging the strap back up. "I love all of this, Nell. I wish I had more time here in Snow Valley, so you could teach me everything you know about working with leather."

"I thought you just sold handbags for Touché," Nell said, a bit confused.

Bethany took in a deep breath. "I do, but I've always wanted to design my own." She looked down at the sketch pad that was in her other hand and walked back over to Nell. "If I show you something, will you be honest with me?"

"Painfully," Nell teased.

Bethany handed her the pad. "Open this and you'll see the handbag designs I've sketched while I've been here. I have more of them back in the city."

Nell did as Bethany asked, quietly studying each design. It wasn't until she came to the last sketch that she looked up and spoke. "Bethany, these are exquisite. I would rather have one of these than any Touché bag."

"It's all because of you, Nell. I was inspired the moment I laid eyes on your ornaments."

"And now you've inspired me. Maybe we should start our own handbag company!"

Bethany laughed. "Don't think it hasn't been suggested. Maybe you'd consider making a prototype of one of the designs someday."

Nell's look softened. "I would be honored to."

"I did want to show you something else, but it's really late notice and if you don't have time to make it by Christmas, that's okay."

"I might. It depends on what it is."

Bethany flipped to the last page of her sketch pad and turned it around for Nell to see. "It's what I'd like to give Mrs. Snyder for Christmas."

Nell put her hands on either side of the sketch and held it up in front of her. "Bethany, this would be a perfect gift for her. She would love it."

"You think so?"

"I know so, and I intend to get busy working on it right away."

"I do need to get back to bake cookies with Mrs. Snyder, but, Nell, it's really okay if you can't finish it in time. I can give it to her later."

"I've got all the time I need. Just leave your sketch pad with me and you'll see.

"I will never be able to thank you enough, Nell."

"You can start by having a wonderful time at Winterhaven tomorrow."

"That will be easy." Bethany started toward the door, then turned around with a raised eyebrow. "And in case I happen to meet someone named Eliot, I'll be sure and tell him you said hello."

Chapter Twenty-six

"I'm ready to bake cookies," Bethany said as she walked into the house and hung her coat on the rack by the front door.

"Mrs. Snyder?" she called a little louder when she didn't see her right away. Fear that Mrs. Snyder wasn't feeling well again began to pound in Bethany's chest until she saw her quickly exiting her bedroom.

"I'm right here, dear," Mrs. Snyder said, producing a wide grin. "I must have been so carried away wrapping presents, I didn't hear you at first."

Bethany released a breath of relief through a grin that mirrored Mrs. Snyder's. "Are you wrapping one for Joe?"

"It's too close to Christmas for those kinds of questions," she answered with a wave of her finger. "The dough should be chilled enough now. Shall we sing along with Bing while we roll it out?"

"That's a great idea," Bethany said, enthusiastically heading toward the stereo to find the album. By the time she returned, Mrs. Snyder had a pastry cloth spread on the counter with a bowl of refrigerated cookie dough beside it.

Both of their voices were already singing the words to "White Christmas."

"If you want to flour the cloth and start rolling out part of the dough, I'll get the cookie cutters," Mrs. Snyder said as the line...*just like the ones I used to know*...flowed from the stereo into the kitchen. "Here is an apron for you."

Bethany tied the strings around her neck and waist, thinking about the Christmases she used to know. They included a discounted tree if they waited late enough to get one, and on occasion there was snow. But there was always music, and similar cut-out cookies, she would spend hours decorating. Modest, unhurried, yet special, is what she remembered. Quite different from her recent Christmases in the city where nothing ever seemed to slow down.

After sprinkling some flour on the cloth, Bethany removed a portion of dough from the bowl and picked up the rolling pin. She stopped when she thought it was just the right thickness and looked at the box of cutters Mrs. Snyder had placed beside her. A picture showed the four different shapes that were inside it, a tree, a star, a stocking and a Santa.

"Should we make some of each?" Bethany asked.

"I think so. The children in town know Joe puts out candy canes and cookies right before Christmas and invariably it's the Santas and the stockings that always go first. It's a good thing I'm partial to the tree and the stars," she laughed.

Bethany smiled. "Here we go then."

What was left of the afternoon sped by as she rolled, cut, and baked until there was no more dough left and several pans and racks were filled with cookies. Smelling the sweet scents of vanilla and sugar for so long, however, had made her hungry.

Mrs. Snyder had just finished mixing up the icing and getting out several shakers of sprinkles and colored sugars for decorating. "I believe it's time we take a break."

"I'd be happy to help you cook something for dinner," Bethany remarked at the same time her stomach gave a low rumble.

The sound of the front door opening caught both their attention. "Actually, dinner just arrived," Mrs. Snyder said with a smile. "I knew how busy we would be baking cookies so I called in an order from the café. All we need to do is set the table."

Joe walked into the kitchen carrying a large sack, filling the air with a savory smell as well. "Charlene's pot roast, with all the trimmings. Though seeing all these cookies, I'm not sure where I'm supposed to put it."

Mrs. Snyder took the sack. "Why don't you set the table and sit down while I put the food in some serving dishes."

This time Bethany's stomach could be heard much louder, causing them all to laugh. "And quickly I might add," Mrs. Snyder said.

Talk of the sleigh ride and Winterhaven Farm dominated most of their conversation while they enjoyed Charlene's cooking. No more had Bethany finished eating, however, when she spoke up with renewed energy. "That was just what I needed, and now I'm ready to start decorating our cookies."

Joe stood up from the table and started collecting the dirty dishes. "I can take care of these so you two can get started."

"How about taking turns icing and sprinkling?" Mrs. Snyder suggested.

"Okay," Bethany agreed as they made their way back into the kitchen. She had forgotten how messy, but fun, it was to do, using different colors on each shape. It went faster than expected with the two of them working in tandem, humming as they went along. Once they had finished, she glanced in the bowl and noticed there was some icing left. "Do you mind if I add some extra touches to the cookies?"

"Of course not. You do whatever you'd like," Mrs. Snyder answered.

"As long as you go rest, and then I'll surprise you," Bethany insisted.

"I'll be on the sofa, reading then," she said with a smile.

Bethany tore off a section of waxed paper and formed it into the shape of a cone like she had learned to make in the past. She then filled it with leftover icing and tore the tiniest bit off the tip for a narrow line of icing to come through. As she squeezed, she embellished beards and created borders, snow, and garlands. Then getting a plate, she carried in samples of each design to show Joe and Mrs. Snyder.

"Those are almost too pretty to eat," Joe said, immediately grabbing one and taking a bite.

"Joe Snyder!" Mrs. Snyder scolded.

Joe chuckled. "I did say *almost*."

"I say we all have one, as hard as we've worked on them." Bethany picked up the star to eat, leaving the tree for Mrs. Snyder.

"You're so creative, Bethany, I'm not at all surprised how detailed these are," she said, admiring her cookie. "But I'm afraid everyone will expect them to look like these from now on."

"It just means Bethany will have to come for a cookie decorating visit," Joe said, casting a grin her way.

Bethany responded with a thoughtful grin of her own, then finished eating her cookie. "I think I better clean up and call it a night."

Mrs. Snyder started to join her in the kitchen but Bethany stopped her. "You are to stay right here and that's an order. Joe you keep an eye on her."

"I always do," he said, giving Mrs. Snyder a wink.

It didn't take long to cover the cookies and sweep the fallen sprinkles and sugar off the floor, but Bethany was glad when she was finally able to go to bed. She was tired, though it was a satisfying kind of tired. As she slipped under the covers, she noticed her phone still on the nightstand. It seemed funny how little she missed having it in her constant possession, at times forgetting about it all together.

She wouldn't have picked it up, except that it showed a missed call...from Kenneth no less. Bethany closed her eyes, wondering what to do. While she assumed things were over between them, those exact words hadn't officially been spoken. Maybe that's why he called, to end their relationship for good. Bethany decided the awkward conversation would have to wait until after Christmas when she returned to her life in the city, as odd as that was going to feel.

It had only been a few days ago that she had been content with the hustle of her career and a potential future with Kenneth. They were all she needed or wanted, or so she thought. Since arriving in Snow Valley, however, Bethany wasn't as sure anymore. She had found what she didn't know was missing. Love. The unpretentious, unselfish, unconditional kind. Not for who she could be but for who she was, something she was afraid may never be good enough for Kenneth.

Bethany propped herself up against the pillow and picked up her phone to look at the photos she had taken of Christopher making the bell. She took her time scrolling past each one, almost feeling the chill and the heat of the workshop again as she did. When Bethany reached the last picture she stopped, her eyes captured by Christopher's face as he held up the bell. He looked happy, despite contending his bells weren't as good as his father's. But then, maybe it wasn't so much about the bell, as it was learning to forgive himself.

Chapter Twenty-seven

Bethany awoke with the sound of a sleigh bell lingering in her ears. She knew she must have been dreaming, but the vision of Christopher, ringing it like he had the day before seemed as real as if she were in that very moment again. She lifted her head and picked up her phone to check the time. It was no wonder she dreamed about him. The last picture she had looked at before she fell asleep was still on her screen.

She smiled as she threw the covers back. In a few short hours, she would be on her very first sleigh ride, getting to hear several sleigh bells. Hopefully, ones Nicholas had made.

"Good morning," Bethany said, practically dancing her way into the kitchen. "And a merry eve of Christmas Eve."

Mrs. Snyder was standing by the cookies when she turned and chuckled. "Now, that's the Christmas spirit if I ever heard it."

Bethany sat down at the table with a cup of steaming coffee. "I haven't had this much fun in a long time, and to believe tomorrow is already Christmas Eve. What do we need to do to get ready?"

"Let's see," Mrs. Snyder pondered. "Charlene always prepares the Christmas Day meal that we eat at the cafe."

"What about tomorrow's dinner?" Bethany asked.

"I guess I forgot to tell you. The church always hosts a chili supper after the candlelight service, and then of course, there's always a special visitor for the children," she answered as if it were truly a secret. "I've had to warn him, though, that he may not fit into his suit if he keeps eating our cookies like he has."

Bethany's eyes widened as she scanned the racks. "That may not be all this special visitor won't fit into if he ate all the ones I see missing."

Mrs. Snyder joined her at the table. "He's ornery enough to have, always trying to claim it's the sweets that keep him sweet, but I know differently. He'd be just as sweet a man without them. Fortunately, most of the ones missing are those he took to the store today."

"Maybe we should take some to Father Alan, too." Bethany suggested.

Mrs. Snyder smiled. "He would be delighted, especially knowing you helped make them. We'll fill up a container and give it to him at church tomorrow night."

Bethany felt her excitement for the day begin to surface again. "What time should we be leaving for the sleigh ride?"

"If our ride is at 11:00 and we pick up Christopher on the way, I would say by 10:00 at the latest. I'd much rather be earlier than later, since I've now heard they offer maple spiced donuts and hot cider while you're waiting," she answered.

Bethany jumped up. "I better start getting ready then."

Mrs. Snyder's head swung around toward the clock. "Are you sure? It's still pretty early."

"I don't want to take any chance of missing out on those donuts," Bethany said, grinning as she left for her room.

But the donuts weren't the only reason. She hoped to take a lot more pictures, and she wanted to look the best she could. Mrs. Snyder had loaned her some curlers and a hair dryer, and if she started right away, maybe she would end up with at least a few soft curls in her hair besides the waves.

Bethany layered on her warmest clothes first, then lightly dampened her hair and began rolling it in sections. The next hour was spent directing hot air onto each curler until she ran out of time and had no choice but to remove them. She was thankful they worked better than she expected and with the help of a comb and a few hairpins, was pleased with how her hair turned out. After a quick application of the mascara and tinted lip gloss she kept in her purse, Bethany walked into the living room, ready to go.

When Mrs. Snyder looked up, her eyes were brimming with surprise. "Why Bethany, aren't you a vision of beauty. Not that you always aren't, but there's a glow about you that's different this morning."

"Thank you. The glow is probably just from using the hair dryer for so long," she joked.

Mrs. Snyder seemed to be in thought a moment longer until the edges of her mouth lifted into a smile. "It's almost time for our sleigh ride. Joe should be here any minute."

They both began putting their coats on, grabbing their gloves, hats and scarves and heading out the door as soon as he pulled up. Their first stop, Christopher's. Bethany didn't know why she would be nervous, but she was. Maybe it was because they both had let their guard down, that she felt more self-conscious and vulnerable. She watched out the window as Joe followed Oaktree Lane to the Smith home and saw Christopher waiting for them on the porch. Bethany wondered if Mrs. Snyder noticed a glow about him, too, as he came down the steps to the car.

"Hi," Bethany said as he slipped in the back seat next to her and closed the door.

"We're so glad you could join us, Christopher. Have you ever been on a sleigh ride?" Mrs. Snyder asked.

"I can't say that I've ever had the pleasure," he answered.

"So that's two first-timers we have. Are they ever in for a surprise," Joe said, glancing into the rearview mirror, causing Bethany and Christopher to exchange smiles.

Bethany felt his gaze continue and turned to look at him again. "Have you had a chance to look through your father's records?"

"Not yet, but I promise I will," he answered.

"Okay." Bethany nodded, remembering he didn't take promises lightly, but found herself not needing one to believe him, anyway.

It wasn't but a few miles farther when Joe turned off the road and past the sign welcoming them to Winterhaven Farm.

"I'm glad there's still plenty of snow on the ground," Mrs. Snyder remarked as they wound their way up to the barn area.

"With it looking like more is on its way," Joe added, glancing up to the sky. "As long as it's not a blizzard this time."

Bethany laughed. "You're not in a hurry to get rid of me, are you, Joe?"

Joe laughed with her until he parked and turned off the engine. "The answer to that question, is not in a million years. Now let's go find us some horses and a sleigh."

"And maple spiced donuts," Bethany reminded them. "I didn't eat breakfast this morning, saving room just for those."

Before she realized it, her door opened, and she saw Christopher holding it to let her out. "Why, thank you."

"You're welcome." he said, giving her a curious smile after closing the door. "You look different today, somehow."

Bethany wasn't about to reveal she had spent a solid hour and a half on her hair before they picked him up. "I'm afraid it's the same old me, but I'll choose to take that as a compliment."

Christopher's eyes seemed to shine as he chuckled. "That's good, because I meant it as one."

Joe and Mrs. Snyder were right ahead of them as they entered the barn to get their donuts and cider. A crackling fire, surrounded by stones, large enough to sit on, was waiting for them when they came back out. Enjoying its warmth while they ate and drank, Bethany's eyes searched the farm around them.

"Where is the sleigh?" she asked.

"It should be here any minute," Joe answered, "but I guarantee you'll hear it before you see it."

The anticipation kept Bethany on the lookout for it anyway, and then she heard them. Sleigh bells. Their unique sounds, blending in rhythm with the horses' hoofbeats, heralded the sleigh's approach. She stood up to get a better view, and then gasped. "That's a real sleigh!"

"That might be why they call it a sleigh ride," Christopher teased, standing up beside her.

Bethany tapped his arm with her elbow. "You know what I mean. Some sleighs these days are more like wagons."

Christopher looked down at her to smile. "I know."

By then, Joe and Mrs. Snyder were behind them, watching the sleigh come closer. "They'll give the horses a few minutes of rest after the current riders unload and then we'll be dashing away," Joe said.

Bethany felt her heart racing. "I don't know how much longer I can stand to wait."

"It's nice to see a big-city girl this excited," Christopher laughed.

"I don't know if I really am a big-city girl," Bethany responded, looking at him while questioning the thought herself.

The sleigh, having reached the barn by then, put a stop to any further contemplation. "Do you think I could pet the horses while they rest?" she wondered out loud.

"It doesn't hurt to find out," Joe answered.

As they walked over to the sleigh, the driver looked at them and smiled. "A small treat for the horses, and then they'll be ready for your turn."

Remembering what Nell had mentioned to her the day before, Bethany got up the courage to ask, "Are you by any chance, Eliot?"

"I am," he answered, somewhat perplexed. "I'm sorry, but I don't know your name."

"It's Bethany. Nell asked me to say hello," she said, fully aware it had been her idea, not Nell's.

Eliot's face brightened. "So, you're a friend of Nell's?"

"Yes, though we've just recently met," Bethany answered with a smile. "Would it be all right to pet the horses?"

"If you're a friend of Nell's, I'll even let you feed them if you want. Just grab a handful of grain from the bucket and open your hand out flat. They won't bite," he offered, gesturing toward the bucket. "It might be easier if you take your glove off."

Bethany had never been this close to a horse, but if she was willing to pet them, she may as well feed them. She did just as Eliot instructed while the others watched her.

"It tickles," she giggled as the horses' soft lips gently lifted the grain from her skin.

Once she had given each of the horses a couple of handfuls, her hand moved to stroke their smooth necks, all the way down to their bell covered harnesses. Bethany took a closer look at the bells, attached to the leather in graduating sizes from smaller to larger. That's when she saw the initials. Father Alan had been right. Winterhaven Farm had purchased them from Nicholas.

Her eyes turned away to meet Christopher's, and she motioned him over. "Look, your father made these," she said, hoping he would be inspired.

His expression was both pensive and proud as he reached out and touched one.

"All aboard," Eliot called, unknowingly interrupting the moment.

Christopher swung his arm out and smiled. "Your chariot awaits."

Bethany laughed as they walked back around to join Joe and Mrs. Snyder.

"Front seat or back seat," Joe asked.

"How about the back?" Bethany looked at Christopher to confirm.

With a nod, he helped her step up, while Joe assisted Mrs. Snyder.

Once they were settled in the seat and covered with the blankets, Bethany leaned over to Christopher to whisper, "Nell hasn't admitted it yet, but she's sweet on Eliot and I'm pretty certain, the feeling is mutual."

"So, part-time matchmaker, too?"

"If two people are meant to be together, they should be together, even if they do need a little push."

"Is that right?"

Bethany turned to him to answer, but her words got lost in his amused expression. She nodded and turned away, needing first to slow down her rapidly beating heart. By then they were on their way, and she didn't need words. The jingling said it all.

Chapter Twenty-eight

Bethany was sorry when the barn come back into view and Eliot drove the horses around the last bend of the trail, signaling her first sleigh ride was about to come to an end. Obliging Joe with a couple of verses of Jingle Bells and modifying the words to sing "a two-horse open sleigh" had truly kept them laughing all the way until now. A contented quiet, warmed with blankets and accompanied by the steady sound of the bells, had taken its place. Bethany took advantage of the moment and pulled her phone from her pocket.

"Smile," she said, leaning closer to Christopher and holding the screen in front of them. After a couple of shots, she turned to face him. "Thank you. I just want to make sure I never forget how special this was."

"That makes two of us," he responded softly, still holding onto his smile as the sleigh came to a stop.

"I want to take a few more pictures so stay put for a minute," she said first to Joe and Mrs. Snyder. "That includes you and the horses, Eliot."

Christopher was already out of the sleigh, helping Bethany down. She quickly took as many pictures as she could of Joe and Mrs. Snyder in the seat in front of them, Eliot in the driver's seat, and of course the horses, dressed in their harnesses and sleigh bells. Once she had finished, she asked Eliot to take one more picture of the four of them together.

"Thank you for everything, Eliot," Bethany said as he returned her phone.

He smiled. "Thank you all for coming to Winterhaven. It's been lucky for us to get this much snow."

Bethany couldn't help thinking Winterhaven wasn't the only ones who had been lucky. They were starting to walk away when Eliot's voice stopped her.

"Oh, Bethany." He waited until she turned around to continue, "When you see Nell, would you tell her I said hello back?"

Bethany nodded. "I'd be glad to."

When they had walked a little farther, Bethany looked up with half a grin at Christopher. "I told you I thought it was mutual. Now, I know for sure."

Christopher looked questioningly at her. "You got all that from two people wanting to say hello to each other?"

Bethany half rolled her eyes as she shook her head.

"Women's intuition," Mrs. Snyder helped to clarify, giving Bethany a knowing look.

Joe chuckled. "Do yourself a favor, Christopher, and don't even try to figure it out. How about finishing off our morning with lunch instead?"

"That's a great idea. Would that be all right with you two?" Mrs. Snyder added, glancing from Christopher to Bethany.

Bethany answered first. "I could always go for some more of Joe Jr's soup."

All eyes were waiting on Christopher when his mouth formed a grin and he shrugged. "I'm in."

"I say, let's go then," Joe said.

Bethany breathed in deeply while her eyes surveyed the scene around her one more time. While photographs were nice to have, they only captured a small, still, piece of the experience. There was so much more to this place that she wanted to remember. Not the least of which were all the mingling aromas of pungency and spice, the farm provided.

Fortunately, there was no waiting to sit down at a table at the cafe. Charlene came right over with an order pad as usual. "Aren't you all a welcome sight. How was your sleigh ride?"

"It was wonderful," Bethany answered with a sigh. "and Eliot was the perfect driver."

Charlene paused her pen to glance up. "That boy is like family to us."

Joe leaned back in his chair with a laugh. "Don't worry Charlene. A little more nudging from these two, and he will be." He pointed a finger at Mrs. Snyder, and then Bethany.

"Well, they have my blessing to nudge all they want," Charlene responded. "Now, what can I get you all to eat?"

"I'll take the chicken and wild rice soup, if you have it," Bethany said.

"The same for me as well," Mrs. Snyder added.

"Joe Jr. created a winner with that one. I believe there's just enough left," Charlene said, writing the order down before looking at Joe and Christopher. "And?"

"A patty melt for me," Joe said with an eye on Christopher. "If you've never had one, I promise your life will never be the same...in a good way."

Christopher didn't hesitate. "With a recommendation like that, I'd be foolish not to try it."

"Coming right up. I'll bring some coffee out while you're waiting," Charlene said before darting off to the kitchen to place the order.

Charlene hadn't been wrong. Within minutes of getting their coffee, she was back at their table with a tray, placing plates and bowls of food in front of them. The smells were intoxicating, especially the one coming from the caramelized onions on the patty melts.

"You're right about these sandwiches, Joe. I can't believe I've never eaten one before," Christopher said after a couple of bites.

"Stick with me…" Joe started.

"And you'll gain twenty pounds," Mrs. Snyder cut in with a laugh.

"Worth every one of them," Joe defended himself as the rest joined in.

Charlene had come over to refill their coffee when the phone by the register started ringing. "Some days it never rings and some days it never stops, but you won't hear me complaining when it does…especially if it's another holiday order."

Bethany smiled as she watched Charlene hurry over to answer it, though anyone calling The Daily Bread would know to let it ring several times. Something changed in Charlene's demeanor, however, that made Bethany suspect it wasn't a holiday order after all.

Charlene walked back to their table after she hung up, her eyes gently targeting Bethany's as she did.

"Was it another order?" Mrs. Snyder asked.

Charlene's focus immediately shifted at the sound of the door opening. "No, not this time."

Bethany turned her head to see who had entered the café and froze in disbelief as Kenneth began walking straight toward her. "Kenneth? What are you doing here?"

"Is that the best greeting you have, after driving all this way to find you?" he asked. "I tried to call, and even left you a voicemail."

Bethany did remember ignoring his call, but never would she have guessed his plan to come to Snow Valley was the reason for it. She pushed her chair back and stood up. "I'm just so surprised to see you." Though it felt a bit awkward, her arms responded to his hug.

Joe got to his feet. "Let me get an extra chair so you can join us."

Christopher stopped Joe before he had the chance. "I have some business calls to make so that won't be necessary. Thank you for a wonderful time today." Then with a quick nod, "Good-bye, Bethany."

Bethany watched Christopher exit the café. The finality in his voice and the dismissal in his manner, caused her heart to ache. She wanted so much to run after him, but what would she say? She would have to admit she had feelings for him that he may not have for her. Besides that, his mind was already made up to leave Snow Valley forever, anyway.

Her eyes turned back to Kenneth with the sinking realization that while they had made a few plans together, that was all they were. If she had learned anything in her time in Snow Valley, it was that real love wasn't something you could plan.

Chapter Twenty-nine

Joe motioned to the now empty chair. "Please have a seat, Kenneth. May we order you something to eat or drink?"

"Just some coffee would be great, thank you," he answered, sitting down where Christopher had once been.

Bethany returned to her chair still stunned he had driven to Snow Valley to see her. As upset as he was over missing their trip, she thought their relationship was over.

Joe didn't even need to summon Charlene to their table. She was already approaching Kenneth with an extra mug. "Let me know if I can talk any of you into a slice of pumpkin or lemon pie?"

"And you wonder why I've gained twenty pounds," Joe commented, throwing his thumb in Charlene's direction as she walked away.

Suddenly remembering her manners, Bethany realized she hadn't made any introductions. "Kenneth, I'd like you to meet Joe and Mrs. Snyder. They're the family I've been fortunate to stay with."

Kenneth nodded. "It's nice to meet both of you. Thank you for taking such good care of her."

"It's nice to meet you Kenneth, but believe me, the pleasure has been all ours," Mrs. Snyder said, smiling at Bethany.

Bethany returned the smile, despite the pang of guilt for wishing Christopher was still the one sitting beside her, not Kenneth. "How did you know where to find me?"

"It was easy," he answered, his tone and expression both dismissive. "All I had to do was ask the man in this little country store I stopped in. He made a phone call, then directed me here."

Bethany and Mrs. Snyder exchanged knowing glances. The phone call Charlene had answered was from Joe Jr.

"How long will you be staying in Snow Valley?" Mrs. Snyder asked.

Kenneth appeared taken aback by the question. "Oh, I'm not staying. I came to talk Bethany into coming back to the city and celebrating Christmas with my parents. There isn't any reason for her to stay here, now that the roads are fine for traveling."

"In that case, you ought not wait too long. The weather can be a bit unpredictable here in the mountains," Joe said, standing from the table. "If you'll excuse me Kenneth, I need to get back to that little country store you spoke of."

"And I should go by the church to make sure everything is ready for the chili supper and candlelight service tomorrow. You're welcome to go to the house where it's more comfortable to discuss your plans. Just let me know what you decide." Mrs. Snyder said, seeming to struggle with the words.

A Sleigh Bell Promise

As soon as they had left the café, Bethany turned to Kenneth. "I think we should take Mrs. Snyder up on her offer."

"That's fine by me," Kenneth said.

Within minutes, they were walking through the front door of the Snyder's house. Bethany loved the first, scented breath she took each time she entered. "Doesn't the Christmas tree smell wonderful?"

"I think the smell of trees is better left outside myself," Kenneth remarked as his eyes scanned the room. "But I'll admit it does feel cozy in here."

"Joe and Mrs. Snyder are such kind people. I wish you hadn't said there was no reason for me to stay."

"It's the truth, isn't it? Besides me being in the city, that's where your real life is."

The words *real life* grated in Bethany's ears. Since being in Snow Valley, she had discovered a life more real than anything she had ever experienced in the city. Joe and Mrs. Snyder were all the reason she needed for wanting to stay. "Maybe I need some time to sort a few things out."

"That's more important than spending Christmas with me? If it hadn't been for your choosing the worst time to fulfill a silly promise, we'd be on a cruise right now, remember," Kenneth's voice rose slightly.

Bethany looked into the eyes she thought she had been in love with, and kept the answer to herself. There had been nothing silly about the promise. The mystery surrounding the bell and her mother had easily become more important to her, as well as the new people that had come into her life. She didn't know why, but her heart was telling her she hadn't chosen the worst time to come but the best.

"I'm sorry the cruise didn't work out and ruined any plans you might have made," she said, still wondering if he had intended to propose.

"My only plans were to have a nice vacation and get to know my boss better at the same time," he responded.

It took a moment for Bethany's mind to process what she had just heard. "Am I understanding you correctly? Did you book us on the same cruise as your boss?"

"I didn't see why not." Kenneth paired his answer with a nonchalant shrug. "I was hoping to pitch some new ideas to him that might help my chances for the promotion, while you could get to know his wife better."

Bethany was flabbergasted. "You were going to tell me this when?"

"Sometime before we got on the ship. It was really no big deal," Kenneth continued without a hint of misgiving.

She stared at him with increased intensity, astounded by his presumption. "So, you were never planning on proposing, were you?"

Kenneth threw her an odd look. "Propose? In the future maybe, but with both of us trying to advance our careers, I hadn't seen a reason to rush into anything. You did promise you'd love me forever."

After the twinge-worthy reminder of her previous use of *promise*, her shoulders dropped. "And you never made the same promise back."

"It should have been obvious I felt the same way about you." His voice disclosed a tone of impatience.

Bethany lowered her head, chiding herself for being so blind. She had chosen to see only what she wanted to in

Kenneth. By the time she raised it, she had made a decision. "Do you know anything about brass?"

Kenneth's face skewed with confusion. "It's a type of metal. What else is there to know?"

After a deep breath, Bethany gave him a pensive smile. "It's actually an alloy composed of copper and zinc. When those two metals are combined, you get a material that is stronger and more malleable."

"Why the science lesson?" he asked, his confusion growing.

Bethany spoke from the memories that were still vivid in her thoughts. "I had the opportunity to watch brass being melted, and then poured into a mold to cast a sleigh bell. It was fascinating to get to see something created that is both beautiful and enduring."

This time Kenneth raised his voice. "What's gotten into you? If this is some kind of test or riddle, I don't get it."

Bethany released a soft grunt. "To be honest, I'm not sure. All I know is we are not copper and zinc. We would never make a good alloy."

Kenneth paused as a frown captured his face. "Is this some strange way of saying you're breaking up with me?"

"We had some good times together, Kenneth, and I don't regret any of them. But, deep inside, we both know I'm not the right one for you."

"This is really what you want?"

Bethany nodded. "You can leave my suitcase at my apartment, or I'll get it from you when I'm back in the city."

Kenneth looked away, the stiffening of his neck suggesting more of a bruised ego than hurt feelings. When he turned back, his expression was coldly indifferent. "It's still in my trunk from the day you left. I'll get it for you."

Bethany watched from the door as he retrieved it. If she had entertained any doubts about letting him go, they were now gone. She met him on the porch as he climbed the steps.

"I guess this is good-by," he said, setting the suitcase down.

Bethany caught his hands and held them for the final time. "I wish you only the best, Kenneth. Merry Christmas."

He only shook his head and left, glancing back once as if he wasn't sure what had just happened.

Bethany hardly knew herself, but only waved before taking her suitcase with her into the house. She was in no hurry to open it. She had already been given everything she needed...and more.

Chapter Thirty

Bethany carried her suitcase into the bedroom and returned to the sofa, contemplating how much her life had changed since she had been in Snow Valley. While she felt a touch of sadness for ending her two-year relationship with Kenneth, staying with him would have been a huge mistake. No boyfriend was worth holding on to if he wasn't the right one. It simply took being stranded in a snowstorm to realize that he wasn't.

She glanced at the clock, wishing she knew when Mrs. Snyder would be home. Having gone from one of the best days of her life to one of the worst, she didn't really want to be alone in the house for the rest of the afternoon. Her first impulse was to drive to Christopher's to tell him that Kenneth was gone for good, both from Snow Valley and her life. Then again, what if he didn't care, what if she had misread the times they had spent together.

She stood up and decided to take a walk instead. Bethany hoped Joe was right and there would be a fresh blanket of snow for Christmas, at least enough to cover all the old footprints and provide a blank canvas for new ones to be made. Not unlike what she hoped would happen with the old footprints Kenneth had left on her heart.

Bethany was heading toward Joe's store when she looked down the intersection toward Nell's shop. Her steps changed course and she began hurrying in that direction. After all, she did have a message from Eliot to return. Though the lights were on, the door was locked when Bethany tried to open it. She knocked to get Nell's attention, and waited a few moments to be let in.

"I hope I'm not interrupting your work too much," Bethany said, stepping inside.

Nell grinned. "Not at all, I'm glad you stopped by. I only locked the door because of a surprise project I need to finish, and I didn't want to take the chance of anyone seeing it."

"If that means you need more time to make the gift for Mrs. Snyder, you know I'll understand," Bethany said.

"That might be true for someone who doesn't know the elf secret," Nell responded with a wink. "I've loved every minute of making it, not only because it was your design, but also because she's been like a second mom to me."

Bethany bit her lip in thought. "It's too bad she and Joe never had children. They would have made wonderful parents."

Nell's eyes seemed to lose some of their initial brightness. "But they did…"

Bethany was quiet, caught in the memory of what Mrs. Snyder told her the night she became stranded in the storm. When she assumed the bedroom had belonged to one of their children, Mrs. Snyder said they didn't have any.

"They had a daughter," Nell continued to explain. "Only there were complications with the pregnancy, and she didn't survive. It was particularly hard on my mother since I was supposed to have been born first."

"They were expecting at the same time..." Bethany's voice trailed into a whisper.

"Yes, as best friends, dreaming of their children growing up together in the same way," Nell finished.

The weight of Nell's words pressed heavily against Bethany's already exposed heart. "So, she would have been my age, too."

Nell nodded. "I was told Mrs. Snyder poured herself into working at the church and opening the closet a few months later. Besides helping my mother with me, her healing came from helping others and making this community her family."

Bethany had a difficult time finding the right words to say next. It made losing Kenneth so trivial compared to what Joe and Mrs. Snyder had been through.

"Now before I lock the door again and get back to work, you must tell me about the sleigh ride and a certain someone," Nell said, her face lighting back up.

"Oh, you mean the certain someone named, Eliot, the owner's very cute son. Yes, he was our driver, and he did want to make sure I told you hello back," Bethany said, not surprised to see a blush of color rise to Nell's cheeks again.

"Thank you for telling me, but you know the certain someone I was referring to wasn't Eliot. Does the name, Christopher Smith, ring a bell?" Nell emphasized.

Bethany tapped her chin in mock thought. "You're right, he did go on the sleigh ride with us, didn't he?"

Nell crossed her arms with a playful glare. "I don't have all day now."

"Okay, okay," Bethany said, beginning to blush herself. "It was wonderful time, I'll never forget, especially getting to hear the sleigh bells his father had made. But then…" she paused with a sigh.

"Then…what?" Nell's eyes widened. "You can't stop there!"

"We went to the café afterwards for lunch," Bethany completed the sentence with a grimace.

Confusion spread across Nell's face. "Wasn't that a good thing?"

"It was until an ex-boyfriend unexpectedly walked in." Bethany's mouth twisted to the side in thought. "I felt like Christopher and I were finally becoming friends, but when Kenneth showed up, he couldn't seem to leave the café fast enough."

Nell's eyebrows rose. "That does sound awful, but somehow I have a feeling you two are going to be just fine."

"Fine as in…" Bethany asked, unsure what Nell meant.

"Friends, of course. Just like Eliot and me," Nell smiled and started to walk Bethany toward the door. "Be back tomorrow at noon so we can talk more, and I'll have Mrs. Snyder's gift ready for you."

Bethany opened the door to leave, but stopped to turn back around. "Thank you, Nell, for being such a good friend and telling me about Mrs. Snyder."

She would have been content to stay in Nell's shop for hours, but Bethany knew how busy she was. At least she had a few blocks to walk before reaching Joe's store. It would give her a little more time to process what Nell had told her about the loss he and Mrs. Snyder suffered. How devastating that must have been for them.

The bells that rang when she entered the store didn't sound anything like Nicholas's, but they still made Bethany's heart smile.

Joe winked when he saw her coming toward him. "Welcome to my little country store."

Bethany rolled her eyes. "I'm sorry about Kenneth, Joe. I had no idea he was coming."

"Didn't bother me a bit. The store is little and the word country is in its name," he responded with a grin.

"I'm afraid Christopher thinks I wasn't being truthful. I had told him earlier that Kenneth was a former boyfriend, because I really thought he was. And now Christopher is going to sell the place, I'm probably never going to see him again, and even worse, I've given him something I wish I would have kept for myself." Bethany couldn't stop the flood of words from pouring out.

Joe's look was sympathetic. "Maybe Christopher just needs to hear you explain it to him."

Bethany wasn't as confident. "He appears to be the stubborn kind. What if he refuses to listen to me?"

"Then we'll just rope him and keep him hogtied until he does," Joe Jr. said, walking up to join them.

"What Joe Jr. said," Joe confirmed with a toss of his head.

Bethany burst out laughing at the vision of them doing just that. She hadn't realized Joe Jr. was in the store as she recounted her story, but looking at the two men ready to come to her defense, filled her with a comfort she'd never experienced before. Bethany couldn't help but believe everything was going to turn out okay with them on her side.

Chapter Thirty-one

"I guess I better be off to the church to see if Mrs. Snyder is still there. Can you two stay out of trouble? Santa's still watching you know," Bethany teased.

"I can if he can," Joe answered, throwing a glance toward Joe, Jr.

Bethany shook her head. "Sounds like trouble, then. See you back at the house."

She left the store, unsure when she should try to speak with Christopher. Part of her was anxious to try right away, but there was a stronger part, telling her to wait. That wasn't going to be easy.

Halfway to the church, however, it dawned on her, that while Santa was still watching Joe, she didn't have a present for him yet. Passing by the bank and the fire station, Bethany slowed down as she walked in front of the next window with the name Antiques and Such painted on the glass. Through it, she could see an assortment of all kinds of items, both old and new. Without any more time or options, she decided to go inside. At first, she didn't see anyone, customer or proprietor, and slowly began to look around on her own. Her eyes could hardly comprehend all they saw, from home furnishings to wall décor to a number of various items in between.

"Needing to find a last-minute gift?"

Bethany jumped as her head swung around to see a much older gentleman, with slightly disheveled gray hair and thick oversized glasses halfway down his nose. She smiled, "How did you guess?"

"Other than I'm about ready to close up shop for the holidays, you appear a little lost. I don't believe I've seen you in here before," he answered.

Bethany grinned. "You're a good observer."

"Can't be in this business for as long as I have and not be," he responded. "I'm Max if I can be of any help you to you."

"Nice to meet you Max, I'm Bethany," she introduced herself, and then thought of Joe's deck of cards. "Actually, do you have anything with Norman Rockwell pictures on it?"

"I'm sure I have a mug and a figurine or two somewhere around here." Max was quickly off to start scouting shelves and cases for them.

Bethany hoped they would be something she liked, but when Max returned with the items in his hands, she looked at him and shook her head.

"There is one more item, if I can find it," he said, taking off again.

She continued walking slowly through the store, scanning the walls where several mirrors and pictures hung. Bethany suddenly stopped. "Max?"

The shuffling sound of Max's footsteps picked up speed as he headed back to answer Bethany's call, his hands empty this time. His eyes followed to where she was pointing.

"There it is," he remarked. "I came across it and a similar one the other day while I was searching through a box. One sold yesterday, and I forgot I had hung this up in its place."

"Well, it's perfect Max. I'll take it," Bethany said unable to take her eyes off the framed print of the exact same picture as on the deck of cards. If it was hanging on a wall in their house, Joe and Mrs. Snyder would be able to see it all the time.

Bethany paid for the picture and watched Max wrap it up for her. Thankfully, it wasn't too large and she would be able to carry it into the church somewhat inconspicuously. "I'm so glad you had this, Max. I hope I can come back and shop when I have more time. Merry Christmas."

She left the store and waved as he flipped the sign over from *Open* to *Closed*. Bethany's steps quickened as she turned the corner to the church and hurried through the door to the offices. Neither Mrs. Snyder nor Father Alan were there. If it weren't for the smells, coming from the kitchen, she would have tried the closet next.

Their voices gave them away before she even saw them, along with a chorus of laughter from several others. Bethany peeked in to catch the eye of Mrs. Snyder and motioned for her to come out. "I'll be right back," she heard her tell them.

"Bethany, are you okay? Joe let me know you were on your way here by yourself, but that was a while ago." Mrs. Snyder's eyes held steady on hers.

Bethany nodded, then sheepishly lifted up her sack. "I had a little shopping to do on the way, but no peeking now."

The corners of Mrs. Snyder's mouth rose. "Hmm...I see you've been to Max's store," she said before her words became more hesitant. "But what happened with Kenneth? I mean...you didn't follow him back to the city?"

"No," Bethany said, looking into the eyes that had done nothing but bathe her in warmth and concern, "because I would have been leaving my heart behind with you and this town. I didn't need any more proof that Kenneth wasn't the one for me. I think I was just too afraid to admit it."

Mrs. Snyder gave her a hug then looked at her more curiously. "Are you sure there wasn't another reason you wanted to stay?"

Bethany briefly turned her head. "It doesn't matter anymore. Christopher is about to leave Snow Valley, so I'm afraid I'll never know what could have been."

"Why don't you put an apron on and help us prepare the chili for tomorrow. Cooking has a tendency to take your mind off things, especially when Doris bursts into song or Father Alan tells one of his Christmas jokes," Mrs. Snyder recommended.

"An apron it is," Bethany forced a smile, walking beside her into the kitchen. After boisterous greetings from everyone, she found a place out of the way to store her coat and gift for Joe, and then tied on the apron Mrs. Snyder had provided her.

"Hey, Bethany, how can Santa deliver presents during a thunderstorm?" Father Alan immediately asked.

Bethany had already started laughing from the groans she heard around her. "I have no idea."

"Because his sleigh is flown by *raindeer*," he answered

Her laugh grew as loud as the groans did. "Good one, Father Alan"

"Don't encourage him, Bethany," Doris said, causing the laughter to continue.

Once they were finished with all the chili preparations, Bethany realized Mrs. Snyder had been right. Between the cooking, singing and joke telling, the time had passed quickly without a thought to what else had taken place earlier that day, both the good and the not so good.

"Shall we go home and fix ourselves something easy for dinner? Joe will be there shortly, as ready to eat as he always is," Mrs. Snyder said.

"I almost feel like I've already eaten after cooking and smelling chili all afternoon, but I'm sure I'll be hungry…especially for a Christmas cookie," she answered.

It was dark as they drove home, but the lights on the houses and the Christmas trees, twinkling through the windows inside them, brought the streets to life. The only thing that could have made it better was viewing it all from a horse-drawn sleigh, accompanied by the sound of sleigh bells. She took one more wistful look around her before following Mrs. Snyder into the house.

"It's been quite a day hasn't it?" Mrs. Snyder commented with a knowing gaze.

Bethany nodded. "One of the best days ever. Thank you again for the sleigh ride. I'll never forget it."

"You do know Winterhaven offers them every year when there's enough snow. I predict many more sleigh rides in your future if you come to visit," Mrs. Snyder said.

"You mean *when* I come to visit, not *if*," Bethany corrected her with a smile.

Mrs. Snyder had removed her coat and was hanging it on the rack when the headlights from Joe's pickup could be seen pulling into the driveway. "Joe must have closed up early tonight. I guess I better see what I can whip up to eat."

"And I better go hide this present," Bethany added, hurrying to take it to her room.

Joe was opening the door at the same time Bethany was back in the living room taking off her coat.

"Looks like you dropped something," he said as she was hanging it up.

Bethany saw him reaching for a piece of paper on the floor and automatically assumed it was the receipt Max had given her.

"That's okay, Joe, I'll get it." Her hand swooped down to pick it up before he had the chance, and she hurried to hide it behind her.

"Got a secret, huh?" Joe winked.

"There are no such things as secrets at Christmas, just temporary mysteries," Bethany said with a wink right back to him.

Joe laughed. "Well, there's one temporary mystery I'm hoping to solve right now, and that is what's for dinner."

"I'll join you in the kitchen in a minute," she said, heading back toward the bedroom.

Bethany was relieved Joe hadn't gotten to the receipt before she did, knowing Max had included a description of the print on it. She should never have put it in her coat pocket to begin with and opened her purse to find a more secure place.

The paper was folded, but she was suddenly aware that it looked much different from what she remembered Max handing her. Unfolding it confirmed her observation. The paper wasn't a receipt at all, it was an old typewritten poem. A tingling chill swept over Bethany as she sat on the edge of the bed and began to read.

The Bell Maker's Poem

Like each new snowflake falling,
Cast by nature to the ground,
This sleigh bell that I give you,
Bears its own unique sound.

Born from heat and molten brass,
Then poured in a sand-packed mold,
Polished last with cob becomes
A treasure of shined gold.

May its ring always usher,
Songs of hope into your heart,
Leaving riffs of timeless joy,
Never again to part.

The bell is yours forever,
Though in case you ever find,
You'd like to share its wonder,
With others of mankind.

Return it to this maker,
For a gift on Christmas Eve,
To one who needs to hear it,
To once again believe.

Nicholas Smith

It took a moment for Bethany to catch her breath. The poem must have been in one of the coat's pockets, but how long had it been there? And how had it not fallen out before? She read it again more slowly, her fingertips brushing over Nicholas's signature as she came to the end. He had to be referring to his special bells.

Bethany took the paper into the kitchen where Joe was at the stovetop stirring fried potatoes and ham in the skillet while Mrs. Snyder was cracking eggs into a bowl.

"Dinner should be ready in fifteen minutes or so, just as soon as the biscuits are done. Hope you don't mind an egg scramble." Mrs. Snyder turned toward Bethany with a smile that quickly disappeared.

"Bethany, what's wrong?" She wiped her hands before hurrying to guide her to a chair at the table.

"There's not really anything wrong. It's this…" Bethany answered, placing the poem in front of her. "It fell out of my coat."

Mrs. Snyder only had a chance to glance at the paper before Joe sat down beside her. "What is it?"

Bethany watched his response as Mrs. Snyder showed it to him. He finally looked up at both of them. "I've never seen this poem before."

"Would you mind reading it out loud, Joe?" Bethany asked.

"Of course not," he answered, giving her a gentle smile.

The words seemed to hold them spellbound after he finished until Bethany broke the silence. "Now, I understand why it was so important for me to return the bell by Christmas Eve, but I'm also curious what Nicholas meant by 'Polished last with cob…'."

"That would be ground corn cobs. Some say it gives metal it's shiniest finish," Joe answered. "I assume that's what Nicholas used."

Bethany's forehead furrowed as her mind shuffled through her memories of the day Christopher showed her how to make a bell. "Christopher never mentioned using corn cobs to polish the bells." She paused a moment. "Maybe that's it!"

Joe and Mrs. Snyder looked at each other before looking back at Bethany. "Maybe that's what?" Mrs. Snyder asked.

"What Christopher has been missing, the reason his bells haven't turned out like his father's. Maybe it's the corn cob," Bethany said still processing the information. "I need to show him this poem."

Mrs. Snyder placed her hand on top of Bethany's. "How about first thing in the morning. A good night's rest will give you both a fresh start"

Bethany knew Mrs. Snyder was right. It had been a long day, and she was most definitely hungry. She nodded. "Egg scramble and biscuits sound delicious."

Chapter Thirty-two

As tired as Bethany felt she wasn't sure how she was ever going to fall sleep. She had spent a quiet evening working on a puzzle with Joe and Mrs. Snyder, all the while trying to piece together the puzzle in her own life. She had caught Mrs. Snyder staring at the Christmas tree more than once, but since she often did the same, it didn't strike her as anything unusual.

If Nicholas included a copy of the poem with each special bell he made, her mother would have had one. Unless it was accidentally thrown away, Bethany would have remembered seeing it when she went through her mother's belongings after the funeral. She knew the coat had been worn by many others since her mother borrowed it, but she couldn't help thinking this was her mother's copy of the poem, that by some miracle it had managed to remain inside the coat's pocket until now.

While there was a unsolved mystery surrounding the bell, it was clear her mother had been in Snow Valley and had met Nicholas. Thinking back over her years growing up, Bethany was sure the gift of the bell had given her mother hope, even though she couldn't ever remember hearing it. The bigger question still looming was why Nicholas gave it to her. Why did her mother need it?

Unfortunately, no amount of continued speculation was going to reveal the answers she desperately sought, so Bethany attempted to close her eyes and think about Christopher instead. She couldn't wait to show him the poem, but she also couldn't wait to explain to him about Kenneth. He was no longer her boyfriend, for certain this time. Whatever Christopher thought of her, she wanted him to know he could trust her.

Searching for more comforting thoughts to help her sleep, Bethany's mind settled on Winterhaven and the vision of traveling across fields among snow draped trees in a horse-drawn sleigh. The vision must have worked as the alarm on her phone caused her eyes to fly open. It was 7:00 a.m. on Christmas Eve and time to get up.

First on her list of things to do was to get dressed and hurry to the café with the intention of seeing Christopher. Bethany wanted to be there early, just in case he was, and she headed toward the kitchen within minutes, ready to go.

Mrs. Snyder was standing next to the coffee and turned around with a smile. "I thought I heard you get up, and here you are already dressed. Are you excited it's Christmas Eve?"

Bethany returned the smile. "More than I have been in a long time. I hope I didn't interrupt your percolator prayers."

Mrs. Snyder shook her head and chuckled. "No, but I did make sure I said one for you this morning."

"For me?" Bethany questioned.

"Yes, for you." Mrs. Snyder walked over to take hold of Bethany's arms and look at her more closely. "For all that you are and all you will be. You're a special person, Bethany. I'm sure you never dreamed you'd be spending your Christmas in Snow Valley, but Joe and I are mighty glad you are."

Bethany looked into the caring face she had easily come to love. "I'm glad I'm here, too, though I have a sneaking suspicion the snow had it planned all along."

Mrs. Snyder laughed. "You may be right. Do you have time for a cup of coffee before you leave for the café?"

"I think I'll grab a cup there while I wait for him to show up. If he doesn't, I guess I'll have to make another house call," Bethany answered, picking up her purse. "Then I have a couple of errands to run before it's time to get ready for church."

"Bethany." Mrs. Snyder waited till she had her attention. "Good luck."

"Thank you." Bethany grabbed her coat and ran out to her car. A glance at the clock told her she should arrive at the café about fifteen minutes early, and sure enough it was 7:45 when she pulled into a parking space at the front.

It was busier than she expected when she walked in, and it took her a moment to find a small empty table in the corner where she would be able to see Christopher when he walked in.

"You're out and about awfully early this morning." Charlene remarked, promptly pouring coffee into a cup as soon as Bethany sat down. "It's Christmas Eve, I hope you've gotten your list made to Santa."

Charlene's down to earth charm never failed to make Bethany smile. "I wouldn't know what to ask him for. I'm afraid what I want the most, can't be wrapped and put underneath the tree."

Charlene nodded at her with a look of understanding. "Well, it never hurts to ask anyway and there's still time. I'll leave my pen so you can write your wish on a napkin and drop it in Santa's mailbox right over there by the register. Let me know if you want to order any breakfast."

She started to walk off when Bethany stopped her. "Charlene, do you think Christopher will be in this morning?"

"I have my doubts, hon. Word has it he's accepted an offer on the property and is trying to get everything ready to move or sell right after Christmas," she answered.

"Thanks Charlene. I'll give him a few extra minutes in case he does." Bethany kept watch out the windows and on the door every time a customer walked in. It didn't take much longer to realize Charlene was right. He wasn't coming.

Bethany's eyes then shifted from the pen Charlene had left to the napkin dispenser. She supposed Charlene was right. What could it hurt to write down a wish? Though it felt silly at first, she pulled out a napkin, picked up the pen, and began writing.

After folding it, Bethany paid for her coffee and got up to leave. With a hopeful breath, she pushed the napkin through the slot of Santa's mailbox, and turned toward the door, bumping into Charlene as she did.

Bethany was mortified. "I'm so sorry, Charlene. Are you okay?"

Charlene chuckled. "I'm as tough as they come. Just glad to see you got your wish sent. Don't ever stop believing they can come true."

She watched Charlene whisk herself away then shook her head. With a lighter step, she walked out of the café to her car. There was a new fluttering in her stomach she couldn't identify. It may have simply been from hunger, or having to make a house call to Christopher, but she had the feeling it was because of something completely different.

Bethany turned down Oaktree Lane, admiring the view even more so than she had before. The landscape of tall trees had become much more appealing than the tall buildings of the city. Next time she wrote a list to Santa, she would have to include a property like Christopher's on it.

She parked in front of the house, relieved to see the smoke billowing from the chimney, a sign Christopher was home and awake. Giving herself a last-minute pep talk, she climbed the few steps to the porch and knocked. She was poised to knock again when the door opened in front of her. The expression on Christopher's face was as she thought it would be, stoic yet surprised.

"I expected you to be back in the city by now," he said, eyeing her with some skepticism.

Bethany responded with a bit of mock smugness. "Seems you're wrong then because, unless I can be two places at one time, I'm standing right here. May I come in?"

"Since I imagine the question was a mere formality and there would be no stopping you anyway, please do," Christopher said with a sweep of his arm.

She hid her amusement as she stepped inside, but was immediately saddened to see the room filled with boxes in different stages of being packed. Bethany closed her eyes to remember the reasons she was there, then looked directly at him. "First of all, I need you to know I had no idea Kenneth was coming to Snow Valley. He had given me every indication that our relationship was over. But if for no other purpose, his being here at least confirmed I had made the right decision."

Christopher's gaze intensified. "And what decision was that?"

"That Kenneth and I were never right for each other. He wanted something much different out of life than I did." Bethany's eyes shifted away to begin scanning the room. "I still don't understand why you want to sell this place. It has to be filled with so many wonderful memories."

"All except for the one I missed getting to make," he responded with a tone of lingering regret. "But mostly, because it's not practical to keep it."

Bethany's eyes returned to Christopher. "What an interesting word that is. What does make something practical? Is it the cost? Usefulness? It doesn't appear to be a decision of the heart in any case."

Christopher's focus strayed briefly in contemplation of what she had just said. "Sometimes it's better if the heart doesn't get involved."

"Let me guess...because that wouldn't be practical."

"You don't give up easily, do you? Is that why you really came, to continue trying to talk me out of selling?"

"If I thought I had any chance of succeeding, I would have come just for that reason. I would start by telling you how things are often not appreciated until they're gone...but then you already know that. No, I came to set the record straight about Kenneth, and I wanted to give you something your father wrote, you may have never seen before." Bethany pulled the poem out of her pocket to unfold and hand to him.

His face was filled with intrigue as he took it from her and began reading. She watched the movement of his eyes, scrolling back and forth across each line until he reached the end and looked back up. "Where did you get this?"

"It's a little unbelievable, but it fell out of this coat's pocket yesterday," she answered, unsure how to read his reaction.

Christopher held his eyes on her. "I wish I had seen this sooner, but thank you for bringing it by. As you can see, I have a lot of work to do," he added with an abrupt glance toward the boxes.

Bethany wanted to inquire more about the poem and what Joe had told her about the ground corn cobs. It was clear, however, that the conversation was over. She had done all she could.

Starting to leave, she paused with a wistful smile. It didn't appear she was ever going to find the answers she sought. "Well, I hope you'll at least consider coming to the candlelight service at church this evening. There's even a chili supper afterward."

"I'm afraid I won't have time for either. Besides, that I haven't been in years," he responded, barely looking her way.

"Then I would say you are *way* overdue," Bethany said, holding her chin firm. "Merry Christmas Eve, Christopher."

She let herself out the front door, the fluttering in her stomach having since moved to her heart. New, exhilarating, and scary, the feeling was unlike any she could remember having with Kenneth.

Chapter Thirty-three

Bethany drove back toward town amidst an onslaught of emotions. There was no escaping the irony that she was moving on with her life by wanting to spend more time in Snow Valley, while Christopher was moving on by wanting to spend less. She had found a home there while he was selling his. If only her heart hadn't opened up and let him in, the likelihood of never seeing him again would be easier to accept.

She took an extended breath as she turned on the street leading to Nell's shop, taking a chance she would be there. Nell had told her to be there by noon, but that was still hours away, and Bethany was anxious to check on Mrs. Snyder's gift. Not to mention that she hoped visiting Nell would help take her mind off of Christopher and everything else that had recently happened.

Bethany was glad to see the lights were on and watched Nell look up from behind the counter when she pulled up. She waved, then got out of her car and entered the shop, through an unlocked door this time.

"I sure didn't expect to see you this early," Nell giggled, taking a bite from a cinnamon roll.

Bethany threw her a grin. "It's Christmas Eve! I wanted to get my errands done so I'd still have plenty of time to wrap presents and get ready for church."

One of Nell's eyebrows rose with a grin of her own. "I think you'll have more than enough time for that. There was somewhere else you needed to go first this morning, wasn't there?"

Bethany released a sigh. "Remind me never to try and keep a secret around here. You talked to your mom, didn't you?"

"She just mentioned you had been at the café when I stopped by to get this cinnamon roll. Want a bite?" Nell offered.

While Bethany would normally decline, her stomach was letting her know coffee didn't count as breakfast. "Well, they are the best I've ever eaten."

That was all the answer Nell needed to hear before she divided what was left of the roll in half. "Here you go, and when you finish eating it, you can tell me how things went with Christopher."

Bethany ate her portion, pondering how things went herself. "What makes you so sure I went to see him after I left the cafe?"

Nell laughed. "Just a strong hunch from that trail of evidence you left behind, like asking mom if she thought he would show up today, and then leaving when he didn't."

"Guilty as charged," Bethany confessed. "I needed to see him again because I found an old poem his father had written about the special bells he made. I also wanted to make sure he knew Kenneth and I were over for good. Not that he cared, Nell. It seems like he can't wait to leave at the same time I'm wishing I could stay."

"So, you admit you have feelings for him," Nell confirmed.

Bethany knew there was no use trying to hide it any longer. "Even if I did, it wouldn't make any difference. Though I would like to have gotten to know him better."

"He does do business in the city. There's no reason why you couldn't still see him," Nell reasoned.

Bethany shrugged at the suggestion. "I doubt it would work, especially since I plan on coming here as often as I can."

Nell's mouth spread into a wide smile. "Do you have any idea how much I'm looking forward to that?"

"Me, too," Bethany said, returning the smile. "I know it's a lot earlier than you told me to pick up Mrs. Snyder's gift. Should I come back at noon?"

Nell reached below her and placed a box on the counter in front of Bethany. "I actually finished it first thing this morning. I hope it's what you had in mind when you designed it."

Bethany's mouth dropped as she lifted the lid off the box and folded back the paper. "Oh, Nell, this is so much more than what I had in mind." She picked up the sign to take a closer look. "The details and the mounting are beautiful...I honestly believe you could make anything. I wish more people could see your talent."

"I'm so glad you like it. But speaking of talent, here's your sketch book back. I hope you don't mind that I looked through all your purse designs again. They're exquisite, Bethany."

"Thanks, though it's not likely anything will ever come of them."

Nell rested her chin on her hand. "You never know…about most things actually."

"You're right about that," Bethany chuckled. "I look back at where my life was only a few days ago, pushing my career, packing for a cruise, and hoping Kenneth was going to propose. Oddly, here I am not missing any of it."

"Take it from me, sometimes we just think we know what's best for ourselves," Nell said with an air of humility. "Like following a boy to college to study entomology."

Bethany burst out laughing. "You didn't."

Nell skewed her mouth sideways. "I did, but after one semester it became glaringly obvious, he preferred six-legged creatures while I preferred the two-legged kind. No regrets, though. I came home to learn all I could about leather crafting, and I couldn't be happier."

"I'm envious of you, Nell. You're doing what you love, in a place you love, with the people you love."

"It's available to you, too. Think about it."

Bethany nodded, not sure what there was to think about. "I better go get Mrs. Snyder's gift wrapped. I will see you tonight?"

Nell smiled. "You bet. I'll be helping to close the café early to set up for tomorrow's dinner. Then I'll be heading home to get ready myself."

"Until tonight then." Bethany left the shop and drove to the house, thankful not to see Mrs. Snyder's car in the driveway. It made it easier to conceal the gift in her bedroom while she went to the kitchen to get something to eat first. The few bites of Nell's cinnamon roll were long gone, and it was still hours away from the chili supper.

She opened the refrigerator to assess what food there was, and was surprised by what she saw instead. A small bouquet of white flowers was tied together, sitting on one of the shelves. Bethany was just starting to wonder why they were in there when she heard the front door open. She hurried to close the refrigerator, suddenly feeling like she was being nosy.

Mrs. Snyder entered the kitchen carrying a couple of sacks. "I thought I better get some last-minute things from the grocery store before they closed for the holiday. Charlene never wants me to bring anything to the Christmas dinner, claiming it's her gift to us, but she knows I always plan to bring a couple of cheeseballs. Would you like to help make them? There will be lots of opportunities to taste test while we do."

"You had me at taste-test," Bethany answered. "I would have helped anyway, but I am a little hungry."

"Now, you know you're supposed to help yourself to any food we have here," Mrs. Snyder reminded her, unloading the sacks. "I'd be happy to fix you a sandwich."

"That's okay, I can wait for the tasting," Bethany assured her.

"Were you able to catch Christopher at the café to give him the poem?" she asked, setting the ingredients for the cheeseballs on the counter.

Bethany shook her head. "He didn't come, so I drove to his house to take it to him."

"And…" Mrs. Snyder paused.

"I couldn't tell what he thought. He seemed interested while he was reading it, then implied it was too late and practically walked me out the door," Bethany said, ending with a frown. "I did manage to ask if he was coming to the candlelight service before I left, but he said he hadn't been in years and wouldn't have the time."

Mrs. Snyder walked over and wrapped Bethany in a hug. "Whether Christopher Smith shows up tonight or not, you're the best thing that's happened to him. If he hasn't realized it yet, he will."

Bethany saw the glistening of moisture fill Mrs. Snyder's eyes after she released her arms. "The first night I was here, I realized how lucky I was that you and Joe happened to me."

Mrs. Snyder closed her eyes as if to prevent the moisture from flowing, but it didn't help. A stream of tears slipped out anyway, prompting her hands to immediately start searching inside her coat's pockets. "Oh, where's a tissue when you need one?"

"Here," Bethany pulled a napkin from its holder on the table and handed it to her. "I hope I didn't say something to upset you."

Mrs. Snyder finished dabbing her face. "No, these are tears of joy. I just hope you'll understand."

Bethany was slightly perplexed. "Understand what?"

Mrs. Snyder hesitated before looking at Bethany with a tender smile. "How wonderful this Christmas is." Then as if the tears had never happened, she removed a large bowl from the cabinet and set it on the counter. "Let's get these cheeseballs made."

Chapter Thirty-four

"I had no idea how easy it was to make these," Bethany commented as she scraped the last bit of cheese mixture out of the bowl and onto a cracker. "And how delicious they are. I already can't wait for Christmas dinner tomorrow."

"That's why we limit ourselves to a small breakfast of blueberry muffins after we open presents, to make sure we leave plenty of room for all of Charlene's good cooking," Mrs. Snyder responded, placing the finished cheeseballs into the refrigerator.

Bethany kept her eyes turned away to guard them from seeing the flowers again, still waiting for Mrs. Snyder to mention them. She didn't, but her words "open presents" sent Bethany a sharp reminder of what she had left to do. "Do you mind if I use some of your wrapping paper and ribbon before I start getting ready for church?"

"Of course not. All the supplies are right there in the hall closet. But I..." Mrs. Snyder hesitated, "I hope you didn't worry about getting Joe or me anything for Christmas."

The corners of Bethany's mouth widened into a broad smile. "Oh, it was no worry at all. I'll be in my room if you need me."

Bethany gathered the supplies from the closet and closed the bedroom door behind her. She placed the gifts in front of her to look at them another time before she started wrapping. Nell had done such an excellent job on the sign for Mrs. Snyder. It wasn't lost on her that they would make a good team with her designs and Nell's skills. Maybe someday they would be able to collaborate on another project, but whatever the future brought, she was grateful for their friendship.

She finished wrapping Mrs. Snyder's first, then turned her attention to the framed print she had gotten for Joe. It wasn't hard to imagine the two of them being just like the couple in the picture when they were younger. Though she and Christopher hadn't been swishing down a hill on a sled, they had dashed across fields of snow on a sleigh ride.

The thought prompted Bethany to pull up the pictures she had taken at Winterhaven. While they might not look like a picture print by Currier and Ives as the song "Sleigh Ride" suggested, they included what was more important, the faces of people she cared deeply for.

Bethany began humming the well-known Christmas song as she looked at each picture. It was more difficult for her to do than she expected, remembering one of the most special days of her life. She turned off her phone then set the finished presents aside so she could lean back on her pillow and rest for a few moments. It didn't seem as if any time had passed when she heard a soft knock on the door, and then Mrs. Snyder's voice.

"Bethany, are you getting ready? We'll need to be leaving for the church in about thirty minutes."

Ready! Thirty minutes! Bethany grabbed her phone to check the time then jumped up to open the door. "I must have fallen asleep, and here I had hoped to do something nice with my hair."

"Maybe this will help." Mrs. Snyder held out a barrette covered in small crystals.

Bethany took it and turned it in her hands, admiring the sparkling design. "It's so unusual and pretty, where did you find something like this?"

Mrs. Snyder smiled. "There's this old clothes closet in town that has been home to some of the most surprising treasures."

Bethany laughed. "Yes, it has. If this doesn't help my hair, I'm afraid nothing will. Thank you."

"You're welcome. I need a few more minutes to finish getting ready myself so don't hurry too much. Joe will be warming up the truck, and I'll be in the living room when you're done."

After a quick nod, Bethany closed the door and quickly began changing her clothes. She didn't want to keep them waiting on her any longer than necessary. The dark green sweater dress Mrs. Snyder had found, fit her as perfectly as the day she tried it on. A pair of black tights she had picked up at the drug store along with her borrowed boots, completed the picture. All that was left was her hair and a touch of makeup.

Bethany brushed her hair over to one side, hoping it would cooperate while she twisted and pinned it into a side bun. Once it felt secure, she fastened the crystal barrette above it and stepped back to take a longer look. She smiled, more from her feelings than how she looked. Aside from the decorations and shopping, Christmas Eve in the city felt like any other day of the year. It was different in Snow Valley.

With a brush of blush, mascara and lip gloss, Bethany walked into the living room, ready to go. Mrs. Snyder wore a look of surprise as soon as she saw her.

"I look all right, don't I? My hair and my dress?" Bethany questioned, suddenly insecure.

Mrs. Snyder rushed over to her. "You look more than all right, dear, you look absolutely radiant. Joe has made sure the truck is nice and warm, but we better bundle up as well. He said the temperatures have dropped quite a bit this afternoon."

The air that hit them as they stepped outside was proof to what Joe had said. The biting, damp chill made Bethany shiver, but more than that, it reminded her of the snowstorm that stranded her there.

"Will people still come tonight if there's a chance for bad weather?" Bethany asked, once she and Mrs. Snyder were settled in their seat.

"There's not too much that would keep the people of this town from getting out on a night this special, least of all the weather. We're pretty hearty folk here," Joe chuckled.

"And they know they can always get home with Joe leading the way if it does," Mrs. Snyder added.

Bethany kept her eyes on the windshield for any evidence of snow, hoping to see at least some flakes fall again before she had to go back to the city. The thought produced a silent dread, not wanting to think about how soon that time would be. She chose to distract herself by studying the vehicles already parked alongside the church as they drove up, keeping an eye out for Christopher's. He didn't appear to be there, but she hadn't given up hope that he still might.

"Bethany, would you like to go with me to the kitchen while Joe finds a place for us in the pews? I want to make sure everything is all set for the supper and they don't need any help," Mrs. Snyder said while Joe was finding their own parking spot.

"I'd like that," Bethany answered. "Especially since I wasn't able to help out this morning."

Mrs. Snyder eased her concerns. "Don't you mind that. You helped out plenty yesterday, not to mention with the hanging of the greens."

Bethany followed Mrs. Snyder through the church's front door and around to the parish hall, connected to the kitchen. The room looked completely different with all the tables arranged and adorned with red tablecloths and centerpieces of candles, ringed with berries and evergreens. A separate table held all the colorful icings and sprinkles required for a cupcake decorating station and another table was equipped with containers of marshmallows, peppermint sticks and enough crushed candies to inspire any imaginable flavor of hot chocolate.

"This looks wonderful. You all worked so hard this morning," Bethany admired.

"It never really feels like work," Mrs. Snyder responded with a smile, her eyes busy scanning the room while she spoke. "One more check in the kitchen and I'll be ready for us to join Joe."

"Oh, there you are," a frantic voice interrupted.

Bethany and Mrs. Snyder turned to see Doris in her red choir robe, rustling toward them at full speed.

Doris looked directly at Bethany, leaving no question whose attention she was seeking. "Please tell me you'll fill in for us. Kathryn wrenched her ankle stepping down from ladder this afternoon, and I have no one else to take her place. I already have to direct the choir and the organist, and it would be so nice to hear a young voice."

Bethany froze, unsure how to respond to Doris's request. "Thank you for thinking of me, but I've never sung a solo in front of anyone, and there's no time to practice. I'm sorry, Doris, I don't see how I can."

"Oh, darlin', I don't need you to sing a solo, not this time anyway. I need someone to read the lessons. I promise it couldn't be any simpler, and Gwen typed the program in large print, so it's easy to read."

Bethany glanced at Mrs. Snyder for guidance, still not accustomed to hearing her called by her given name.

Mrs. Snyder's eyes were gentle and encouraging. "I know you would do well, but it's up to you."

Her eyes shifted back to Doris. There was no way she could say no to her, besides that it would be a perfect way to give something to the community that had so generously welcomed her. Bethany took in a deep breath. "Let's go before I change my mind."

Doris turned in a hurry, securing her arm through Bethany's as if to ensure she couldn't. "First, we'll find you a choir robe and a program to look over. After all the lessons and carols are finished, Father Alan will give a short homily followed by the lighting of the candles and the singing of "Silent Night." Then watch out because everyone is starving by then," she finished.

Bethany pulled a few choir robes off the rack Doris had led her to and checked the lengths. She quickly settled on one she wouldn't trip on, and then joined the rest of the choir, waiting to process down the aisle.

Looking over the lessons she would be reading, Bethany was able to relax a little and peered inside the doorway at the pews. She made a note of where Joe and Mrs. Snyder were sitting, as well as Nell and her parents. A grin formed when she also noticed Eliot and his family in the pew right behind them. The only other person she hoped to see, but didn't, was Christopher.

Bethany was glad to be walking beside Doris as the first hymn accompanied them to their seats, close to the podium she would be reading from. Her hands began to sweat and her heart began to palpitate, whether because of nerves or the extra warmth of her choir robe, she didn't know. The hymn ended and it was time for her to step up and read the first lesson. Thankfully, the flushed feelings subsided within the first few words she spoke, even after she caught a glimpse of Christopher slipping into the back pew.

Her eyes danced back and forth between him and the Snyders while the lessons and carols continued. Bethany was almost sorry when it came time to light the candles. As beautiful and meaningful as it was, she knew it meant the service was coming to an end. She made an intentional effort to commit the flickering moment to memory while the notes to "Silent Night," began to play.

Bethany's focus remained on Christopher as she watched his candle be one of the last to be lit, and he joined in the singing. She imagined the golden hues in his eyes were even more pronounced with the illumination. He must have felt her gaze, for their eyes met and held on to each other for the remainder of the verse.

She wished she could read his thoughts, but was just happy he came and hoped he would join them for chili. That was until the organist stopped playing and the last verse began with only voices. Christopher blew out his candle and left the pew, creating a small black hole, not only in Bethany's vision but in her heart. In what felt like an instant, he was gone, having extinguished both a light and her hopes in his wake.

Chapter Thirty-five

For a moment, Bethany allowed herself to think that Christopher wanted a head start in line for chili or that he got an important phone call he needed to answer. She was aware, however, that neither was likely true. Christopher was gone, and she had a crushing feeling she would never see him again.

The lights of the church came back on as the rest of the candles were blown out and people began leaving the pews. Bethany was anxious to join everyone in the parish hall, but first she would need to return her borrowed choir robe to the rack.

Doris took her arm as they followed the other members of the choir in that direction. "Oh Bethany, how can I ever thank you. You did such a splendid job of reading the lessons."

Bethany looked at her and smiled. "I was glad I could help."

"Doris is absolutely right."

They both turned around, surprised to see Kathryn hobbling up right behind them with a cane.

"In fact, you did such a good job that I already feel a pain coming on in my ankle for next year. You will be with us again, won't you?" Kathryn asked in her straightforward manner.

Bethany burst out laughing. "I hope to be. On the chance that I am, how about we share the reading?"

Kathryn appeared pleased with the suggestion. "I'm looking forward to it."

"I thought you were supposed to be home, resting your ankle." Doris injected herself into the conversation.

Kathryn waved the concern aside. "I'll have plenty of time for that later, and it wouldn't feel like Christmas otherwise. I just had to promise, Max, I would bring this ridiculous looking cane with me."

Hearing his name immediately caught Bethany's attention. "Max? The same one who runs Antiques and Such?"

"The very same one, bless him. I'm afraid he's not going to stop until he drops. He can't bear to let the shop go, and no one has expressed an interest in taking it over," Kathryn answered. "But speaking of the man, I better go keep a close eye on him. He always overdoes on the sweets this time of year."

Bethany watched Kathryn hobble away, admiring the strong and dignified manner in which she did so. She then turned her attention to Doris. "I would hate to see that shop close."

"As would the rest of the town. We've had our share of ups and downs. Fortunately, more ups than downs, and I do everything I can to keep it that way." Doris accompanied her words of determination by slipping her arm back through Bethany's. "Now, let's go get us some chili."

She steered Bethany into the hallway with zealous steps, almost colliding with Father Alan.

"I should know better than to get in the way of a woman on a mission," he teased.

"Aren't you supposed to already be in the parish hall?" Doris half scolded him.

Father Alan lifted his hands in defense. "I promise I'll be right there, but while I have you here, Bethany, may I speak with you for a moment?"

"Of course," she answered, a bit curious.

"Don't you keep her too long, Father. This is Bethany's first Christmas Eve chili supper," Doris stated before continuing on down the hallway.

"Can you guess who runs the show around here?" he asked, shaking his head.

"Oh, I don't have to guess," Bethany answered with a wide grin. "But does she not have any family here?"

Father Alan smiled softly. "I believe Doris would claim that all of us are her family. I know she was engaged once, but that was a while before I was called to St. Paul's."

"Hmm…I wonder what happened, and why she never got engaged again," Bethany thought out loud.

"I understand there was an accident," he answered. "For some people, having that one perfect mate, no matter how long, is enough to carry them through a lifetime."

Bethany was quiet, his statement having exposed a poignant truth. Kenneth would never have been that one perfect mate no matter how long they were together.

Whether it could have been Christopher seemed destined to remain unknown.

"Ones of the reasons I wanted to speak with you was to see if Nell was able to finish Mrs. Snyder's Christmas gift," Father Alan said.

Bethany nodded. "It's already wrapped and under the tree."

"That's wonderful," he acknowledged. "I can't think of a better way to begin the expansion of the closet along with your idea of selling some of the items, than with an actual sign, named for the person who started it."

"She's helped so many people. I know how happy it's going to make her, to be able to help even more," Bethany responded with a smile.

Father Alan's mouth opened to speak again, but he seemed hesitant as if still needing to gather the right words. "Mrs. Snyder has already been happier than I've seen her in a long time. Not since…"

Bethany reached out to stop him. "It's okay, Father Alan. I know what she's been through."

His chest lifted as he took in his next breath. "Those were such difficult times for them, first losing their own child, and then losing the chance to adopt one a few months later, even though they understood it was for the best."

Bethany's body stiffened as if the wind had been knocked out of her. Nell hadn't mentioned anything about an adoption. While Father Alan's words were stunning, she managed to hide their effect with an affirming nod, not wanting him to feel any more uncomfortable than he already appeared. It was obvious those times had been heartbreaking for more than just Joe and Mrs. Snyder.

"Before you hurry off to the chili supper, I also wanted to say how glad I am you stayed in Snow Valley for Christmas. Not only because of the delicious cookies you helped bake either," he said with a wink. "You've been a blessing to all of us."

She had her doubts Christopher shared the same sentiment, but she appreciated what Father Alan had said. "Thank you. Being here has been as much a blessing to me, if not more," she said, starting to leave.

"Bethany…"

Father Alan's voice caused her to pivot back around. His face bore an expression of bewilderment this time. "I know the reason you came was to return a gift to Nicholas, but something is telling me…the real gift is you."

Chapter Thirty-six

Bethany walked toward the parish hall, her emotions reeling from everything Father Alan just revealed. Nell must not have known about the potential adoption either, or she would have told her. Father Alan didn't say whether the child was a girl or boy, but if it was a girl, it must have almost felt like losing another daughter. She was curious why the adoption fell through, but the most likely explanation was obvious. The mother decided to keep the baby.

The sadness of it all was heartbreaking, making Bethany want to create as much happiness as she could for the Snyders, now and in the future. That was the least she could do for all they had done for her. She was also ready to fill her empty stomach and be a part of the festivities. Entering the parish hall, Bethany saw how easy that was going to be.

She waved at Joe and Mrs. Snyder, already sitting at a table, and went to stand in line for the chili. Waiting, gave her the opportunity to study everyone who was there, on the small chance Christopher had ended up staying. He hadn't, but she saw Doris with Kathryn and Max, enjoying themselves with Kathryn using her cane, less for walking than as a prop for getting her opinions across.

By then, Nell was handing her a bowl of chili. "I'll be ready to join you for cupcake decorating and hot chocolate as soon as you've finished."

Bethany nodded with a smile and took the chair next to Mrs. Snyder. She couldn't imagine Kenneth ever agreeing to spend his Christmas Eve like this, while she could no longer imagine spending it any other way.

She hadn't laughed so hard at her and Nell's cupcake masterpieces nor what they thought would be the ultimate combination of flavors in the hot chocolate. Bethany was sitting down, finishing her last bite of cupcake when she looked at Nell. "Did you know Christopher was at the service tonight?"

Nell shook her head. "Not until Mom and I saw him standing by the parish hall door when we hurried down to start serving the chili."

"It would have been nice if he had chosen to stay and eat," Bethany remarked.

Nell sighed with more than a touch of frustration. "I tried to talk him into it, but he claimed he had too much work left to do."

Bethany had no trouble discerning what that work was. "It sounds like he had more packing to do."

"Maybe," Nell shrugged, "but at least Mom convinced him to take some chili home, and then invited him to our Christmas dinner at the café tomorrow."

The words dared Bethany's heart to hope she might see him again, after all.

Nell tipped her cup back to get the last bit of her hot chocolate. "And now I'm going to have to leave, too," she said with a grin. "This elf has some work to finish up."

Bethany laughed, picturing Nell with pointy ears and shoes.

"Oh, but wait," Nell ran back into the kitchen and returned with her coat and an envelope that she pressed in Bethany's hand. "I almost forgot."

"What is this?"

"I have no idea. Christopher just asked me to give it to you."

Bethany lifted the envelope up to read what was written on the front, immediately recognizing his handwriting. It was the same as the note he had written on the napkin at the café. *Do not open until December 25th*.

"At least you don't have to wait much longer to find out." Nell finished buttoning her coat and pulled on her gloves. "I'll see you at dinner tomorrow."

She guessed Nell was still working on some gifts, possibly even one for Eliot. Watching her leave, Bethany longed for a time she would be able to help her.

Bethany hadn't moved when Mrs. Snyder walked up beside her. "Are you ready to go? We still need to hang our stockings by the chimney with care, you know."

"In hopes that St. Nicholas soon will be there," Bethany added with a smile that abruptly disappeared. "But I don't have one."

Mrs. Snyder's lips were pressed together as her eyebrows rose. "I'm sure we can find an old sock for you to borrow. I'll have Joe pull the truck around for us."

Bethany went to retrieve her coat, and tucked the envelope inside her purse before bundling up to go back outside.

She followed Mrs. Snyder to the front door and gasped as soon as it was pushed open. "It's snowing!"

Mrs. Snyder laughed. "I believe someone's wish was answered."

Bethany was sure she hadn't been the only one to make that wish. She just hoped it wouldn't be the reason Christopher didn't come to dinner at the café.

There was still enough evening left once they got home that Joe started a fire while Bethany took her purse into her bedroom. She went ahead and removed the envelope and placed it on the nightstand for her to open on Christmas Day.

The three of them talked and sang while listening to Christmas music and finishing the puzzle they had begun earlier. It was easy for Bethany to compare the pieces to her own life, especially the ones that looked to be a perfect match, until they weren't. Kenneth. And the place where one piece was still missing, but try as she might, she couldn't find. Snow Valley.

It wasn't too much longer when Mrs. Snyder suddenly got up from the table and left the room, returning with a box. "It's time to hang the stockings."

She lifted the lid and removed them, each one made of the same red wool fabric and white cuff, bearing their names in red sequins. "Bethany, here is yours and, Joe, yours," she said, handing them out before picking up her own. "Now we're ready."

Bethany couldn't believe what she was holding in her hand. "But Mrs. Snyder…"

"I couldn't seem to find an old sock anywhere." Mrs. Snyder shrugged with a grin then led the way to the mantel. She hung hers in the middle, while Joe hung his to the left, leaving Bethany to hang hers to the right.

"Looks like we're ready for Santa, now, so don't you ladies stay up too late and keep him from coming," Joe said. "I'm off to bed in case he calls and needs me to do some plowing for him or his reindeer."

Bethany laughed. "Good night."

She and Mrs. Snyder stood beside each other, admiring them. "Thank you for making one for me, though I don't know when you've had the time."

Mrs. Snyder turned to Bethany and took hold of her hands. "Joe's and mine were finished a long time ago, so I only had yours to do." She closed her eyes before she continued. "Bethany, I need to tell you something I should have already told you."

Bethany suspected it was about the daughter she and Joe had lost, though, it was never something Mrs. Snyder needed to explain. "Are you sure it can't wait until later? It's Christmas Eve."

Mrs. Snyder lightly squeezed Bethany's hands. "That's the reason why I need to."

"How about we sit down first," Bethany suggested.

Mrs. Snyder nodded and joined her on the sofa with a deep breath. "I wasn't honest with you on the first night you stayed with us, but I didn't want to make you feel uncomfortable. So, when you asked if the bedroom used to belong to one of our children, I answered that Joe and I didn't have any. That wasn't entirely true. We did have a daughter, just not for very long. There were complications, and she died soon after she was born."

Bethany could hardly bear to hear the story again. "I'm so sorry, Mrs. Snyder. What a terrible loss you and Joe faced. May I ask what you named her?"

"Her name was Sarah. I hope you don't mind that I put your name on her stocking since I was never able to do it for her."

"It's an honor, Mrs. Snyder. Please don't worry you didn't tell me about Sarah in the beginning. I was just a stranded stranger you were generous enough to bring into your home."

Mrs. Snyder had held her composure until that moment, and then the tears started spilling onto her cheeks. "Oh, Bethany, there's so much more I need…"

Bethany was quick to wrap her arms around Mrs. Snyder to stop her, knowing what more there was and not wanting her to relive any more pain. "There's nothing more important right now than celebrating Christmas together and baking your mother's delicious blueberry muffins. Please, you can tell me later, okay?"

After a moment, Mrs. Snyder pulled back and nodded. "I suppose I better get to bed then, too."

"I'll be heading there shortly, I'd hate to miss out on any visions of sugarplums, dancing in my head," Bethany said with a soft smile.

Mrs. Snyder managed to respond with a smile of her own as she stood up to leave. "Now those would be sweet dreams."

Bethany turned off all the lights except those on the Christmas tree so she could spend a few minutes gazing at its colored reflection around the room and on the stockings. To think Mrs. Snyder had held onto Sarah's stocking all this time, and put her name on it instead, was humbling. She stepped over to them to touch each one. Mrs. Snyder's handwork was undoubtedly skillful, in the way she sewed on the sequins. *Joe*, *Gwen*, and *Bethany* her eyes read, names that would forever be etched in her heart.

She unplugged the lights with a tug of reluctance and got ready for bed herself. As she crawled underneath her covers, she took a long look at the envelope from Christopher. It was almost midnight and officially Christmas Day, but she would wait until the morning to open it. Unlike other people she knew, Bethany never wanted to hurry the opening of gifts. Though the envelope wasn't a traditionally wrapped gift, it produced the same anticipation she loved to savor. What sounded like a sleigh bell ringing in the distance only increased the anticipation, creating the amusing expectation to also hear the prancing and pawing of each little hoof.

With so many thoughts vying for her attention, Bethany doubted sleep would come easily if at all. She rolled over to face the window and watch the snow that was still falling. Bethany wished she would be snowbound again for a number of reasons, not the least of which it would mean Christopher would be snowbound as well. She wasn't ready to leave the Snyders and her new friends and go back to the city, though she honestly couldn't say when she would be.

Nell had made it sound like she had a choice, but she couldn't simply throw away her career at Touché, could she? What else would she do? Bethany's mind contemplated the possibilities while watching the flakes drift downward between the panes of glass. She didn't know enough about antiques to take over Max's shop, even though she was willing to learn, and Joe already had Joe Jr. helping him at the store. Maybe Charlene could use some help at the café, or maybe she could use her marketing skills to help Nell and bring more visitors into the town. Unfortunately, she feared none of her ideas were practical, though she had gotten on to Christopher for using the same measure.

Bethany continued to gaze out the window until as if rocked by the gentleness of a snow lullaby, her eyelids grew heavy and without even realizing it, she fell fast asleep.

Chapter Thirty-seven

The sound of the front door closing caused Bethany to wake with a start. Burrowed under a thick layer of blankets, she listened to the footsteps that followed. While they were softer than usual, Bethany could tell by the length of their stride, they were Joe's.

The bedroom was illuminated with natural light, signaling it was morning, but she sensed it was something more. Bethany slipped out from the warmth to push the curtains aside. A real Christmas snow had covered everything with a fresh coat of sparkling white crystals. Joe must have been out plowing, or helping Santa she mused.

Though fully awake, Bethany crawled back underneath the covers to wait until she knew both Joe and Mrs. Snyder were up as well. There would be no point in trying to go back to sleep as anxious as she was for them to open their gifts. She had always enjoyed giving them more than getting them and hoped the Snyders hadn't worried about having one for her under the tree. Besides the stocking, they had already given her the best gift they could by making her feel like part of their family.

The thought of gifts reminded Bethany of what she hadn't opened yet. She looked at the nightstand to see the envelope from Christopher. While he may not have meant it as a gift, he did stipulate that it wasn't to be opened until Christmas Day, which qualified as one to her. Why she felt so hesitant, she wasn't sure. Maybe it was because she was afraid the envelope contained nothing more than an obligatory note, saying he was glad to have met her and wished her a future of success and happiness. Bethany didn't even know how to define those anymore.

She determined the only reason Christopher wanted her to wait to read it, was because he planned to have already left town by then and could avoid having to face her again. On the other hand, he would have known about the chance of snow and the possibility the roads may be closed.

Her emotions continued to play tug-of-war as she thought back to the times they had spent together. No words of confessed feelings had been spoken between them, but then again, love didn't need words. Bethany couldn't help but wonder how she had gotten it all so wrong.

Tired of useless contemplation, she knew there was only one way to find out. She picked up the envelope and stared at it another moment before turning it over. Her finger had just slid under the edge of the flap when she heard voices, both Joe's and Mrs. Snyder's. That was all the excuse Bethany needed to return the envelope to the nightstand and throw on her robe and slippers. Joining them on Christmas morning was much more important.

"Merry Christmas!" Bethany bounced into the living room, surprising Joe and Mrs. Snyder into laughter.

"And we thought we were being so quiet." Mrs. Snyder stepped away from the fireplace to give her a hug. "Merry Christmas, Bethany."

"I've been awake for a while," she giggled. "Did I hear you come in from plowing, Joe?"

A twinkle appeared in Joe's eyes as he answered. "Santa was fine, but I wanted to make sure I cleared a path for everyone else, coming to the café for Christmas dinner. I'm pretty sure Charlene invites the whole town."

Bethany smiled. "I have no doubt about that."

She then took in the whole picture in front of her, the licks of flames crackling below the now bulging stockings, and the ribbon wrapped packages filling the space underneath the tree. Add in the smells of coffee brewing and muffins baking, and Bethany couldn't imagine a better Christmas morning, in spite of the undercurrents of grief and disappointment she still felt.

"And since it looks like Santa came, I think we should see what he brought us," Joe continued, unhooking each stocking, handing Bethany's to her first.

"I sure am glad he knew where to find me," she joked, waiting to peek until they each had theirs and were sitting down.

"Go ahead, I'm excited to see what you got," Mrs. Snyder said with enough enthusiasm to almost make Bethany believe she honestly didn't know.

Bethany smiled as she pulled out an assortment of candy, lotion and lip balm, until she reached the last item in the foot of the stocking. It was a pair of cream-colored wool gloves.

"I thought those would look nice with your coat," Mrs. Snyder said.

"They'll be perfect. I love them." Bethany immediately tried them on. "I can't wait until the coat is officially mine, though I feel a little guilty no one else will be able to borrow it."

Mrs. Snyder shared a glance with Joe before looking back at Bethany. "That coat has been on quite a journey over the years, but now it's right where it's supposed to be. With you. We already made a donation to the closet for the coat. It's our Christmas gift to you."

Bethany paused from admiring the gloves to jump up and hug each of them. "Thank you. You've done too much for me already." She then retrieved their presents from under the tree. "This means it's time to open your gifts from me. Joe, you first."

Joe grinned as a light shade of embarrassment colored his face when she handed him his. "I wonder what this could be?"

"There's only one way to find out," Bethany answered with teasing impatience.

She watched creases of curiosity deepen across his forehead, then diminish with a smile once he removed the paper and lifted the lid.

"Well, I'll be. Look here, Mrs. Snyder." Joe lifted the picture out of the box and turned it around for her to see.

"Just like the picture on our deck of cards. Where on earth did you find it?" Mrs. Snyder's voice was pitched with astonishment.

Bethany grinned. "Antiques and Such."

Mrs. Snyder took the picture from Joe's hands to take a closer look. "This was in Max's shop? How did I miss seeing it?"

"I'm learning there are all kinds of treasures in Snow Valley one might miss," Bethany answered.

"Yes, there are." Mrs. Snyder's eyes were thoughtful as they remained on the picture before looking up. "I can't wait to see it hanging on the wall."

"It will be, just as soon as we're home from the café," Joe responded and set the picture back inside the box. "Thank you, Bethany."

"You're welcome. It's your turn now, Mrs. Snyder." Bethany held out her gift, biting the side of her lip in anticipation.

Mrs. Snyder laid a hand on top of Bethany's. "You do know there's not a thing you could give me that I wouldn't love."

Bethany nodded while pondering Mrs. Snyder's uncanny ability to read her mind and waiting for her to open the box.

Mrs. Snyder's eyes widened when she folded back the tissue paper to uncover what was inside. She seemed unable to speak.

"I hope you like it. I gave Nell my design, and she made it for me." Bethany felt suddenly insecure.

Mrs. Snyder turned to look at her. "Oh, Bethany, I love it. I just can't believe you did this."

Bethany smiled with relief. "Father Alan and I couldn't imagine naming it anything else."

"Do I get to see what it is you two are talking about?" Joe finally asked, having been unable to catch any glimpses of the gift from where he sat.

Mrs. Snyder first matched Bethany's smile, then held up the embossed and engraved leather sign for Joe to see.

"Gwen's Closet," he read, slowly hanging on to each word. "It couldn't be more perfect."

"Nor this Christmas. It's been one I'll never forget," Bethany added.

Mrs. Snyder was careful to lay the sign back in the box and reach for a small package tucked between some branches. "It's not quite over yet. Here is one more for you, Bethany."

It was Bethany's turn to be curious as she pulled off the ribbon and paper, and removed the top. She could feel her pulse begin to race as soon as her eyes fell on the sleigh bell. She picked it up, confused that it looked to be the exact same one Nicholas had given her mother, down to the initials and the year. Another glance inside the box revealed something else, a folded sheet of paper. Bethany already knew it was a copy of the poem.

She lifted her head. "I don't understand. I gave these to Christopher. Is this his way of giving them back to me?"

Mrs. Snyder gently shook her head. "Nicholas made two bells that year. He said there were two women in need of hope, and he couldn't bear to choose between us. Nicholas gave one to me and one to your mother."

"You never told me." It was obvious by Joe's voice that he hadn't known.

Mrs. Snyder went to put her arm around him. "I tried to several times, but the pain of losing Sarah was still so fresh, and then..." she looked at Bethany and paused, "...and then as the years passed, I didn't want to reopen the grief."

Bethany's mind tumbled with questions. "But it belongs to you, Mrs. Snyder. Why would you want to give it to me?"

"Because I don't need it anymore, and I want you to have it, not only as a reminder of hope, but of love, the most unexpected and real kind of love," she answered, glancing between Bethany and Joe. "Maybe you'll have someone you want to pass it down to someday,"

Bethany stepped forward to put an arm around each of them for a long moment. "And now I believe you two have your own presents to open. Why don't I pour us some coffee while you go ahead?"

She went into the kitchen and paused next to the percolator, calming her thoughts before pulling three cups out of the cabinet. There was welcome laughter coming from the living room as she did. Pouring their coffee first, she carried the cups in to Mrs. Snyder's exclamation. "A collar and a leash? A bone that squeaks? Joe Snyder what have you done?"

Joe grinned. "Nothing yet, Mrs. Snyder, but I'd been thinking it was time we had a dog, and Bethany's gift only confirms it. That picture wouldn't be complete without one, and I think the same goes for our family. He could be the store's mascot or the closet's mascot, or both."

"I can't believe I'm saying this, but I think it's a wonderful idea, Mr. Snyder," she laughed again. "Which makes my present to you even more useful for all those walks you'll be taking."

Joe opened his to find a new pair of boots and smiled. "Looks like we're ready to find us a dog just as soon as the shelter opens back up after the holidays. Right now, I'm ready to eat some muffins."

Bethany's stomach had been growling as she sipped her coffee.

"Why don't you two have a seat at the table and I'll fill a plate with some right now," Mrs. Snyder stood up to head toward the kitchen with Bethany following behind to help and Joe putting on some Christmas music.

Not much was said while they ate until Mrs. Snyder eventually spoke up. "Bethany, I hope you don't mind that Joe and I have somewhere to go this morning before our dinner at the cafe. It's the flowers in the refrigerator. We always put them on Sarah's grave at Christmas."

"Of course, I don't mind." Bethany said. "I'll just be sitting by the fire, enjoying the tree and listening to the music I can't seem to get enough of."

After a quick clean-up and time to get dressed, Joe and Mrs. Snyder were gone, leaving Bethany to do just as she said she would. Sitting on the sofa, however, allowed her thoughts to run rampant, trying to make sense of things. She picked up the bell and jingled it again, never thinking it possible she and Christopher would have matching bells.

The thought reminded her of the envelope she had yet to open. Bethany retrieved it from the bedroom then slipped her finger back into the corner and ran it along the flap, tearing it only slightly as she did. She closed her eyes as she reached in and pulled out a piece of paper. When she opened them again, they caught sight of a smaller piece of paper in her lap that must have fallen out at the same time. Bethany read it first.

I found this in a small black notebook next to the Smith family Bible. I hope it gives you the answers you're searching for. Merry Christmas, Bethany. Christopher.

Her next breath hitched in her throat as she unfolded the larger piece of paper and saw the date at the top, the same year that was engraved on the bell. Bethany tried to continue reading, but could barely get past *For Miriam*, before her vision became so blurry, she had to stop. If a heart could melt, hers was pouring out of her in tears at that very moment.

Chapter Thirty-eight

Once the tears had subsided enough, Bethany dried her face and attempted to start reading where she left off.

"Snowbound and alone, save for this beautiful baby girl, may the ring of the sleigh bell remind her there is always hope no matter how difficult the circumstances may seem. While there is another family, so deserving of adoption and with so much love to share, I pray the joy of this child will serve as a catalyst for Miriam's strength and courage, able to heal the brokenness of her own family. May each time her daughter smiles, her heart will, too, knowing she made the right decision. Love always leaves something beautiful behind."

A prickling chill ran down Bethany's arms. It was her. She was the baby the Snyders were prepared to adopt. What were the chances they would ever meet? A sudden lightness as delicate and wispy as butterfly wings could be felt inside her chest, and she knew. This was her mother's plan all along. Her reason for sending Bethany to Snow Valley was for a far greater purpose than to return a gift. She didn't want her to be alone and had sent her to find the family she may have had, were it not for a bell maker.

It was impossible for Bethany to keep the tears from flowing again. There was no way her mother could have known what the outcome would be, but she made the selfless attempt anyway, to give her daughter one last Christmas gift, one more valuable than any she could have unwrapped.

She wasn't ready for Joe and Mrs. Snyder to return home and find her like this, but the front door opened anyway. It was too late.

"Bethany, what's wrong?" Fear emanated from Mrs. Snyder's voice as she hurried over to sit next to her.

Bethany watched the color fade from Mrs. Snyder's face. "There's nothing wrong, I promise."

Mrs. Snyder appeared to swallow hard. "Then, what is it?"

The paper Christopher had given Bethany was still in her hand. She held it for Mrs. Snyder to take. "Nicholas wrote this on the Christmas Eve he gave you and my mother the bells."

Tears streamed down each of Mrs. Snyder's cheeks as she read it. "Oh, Bethany, I wanted to tell you everything as soon as I realized who you were, but I didn't know how. It all seemed so unreal, I had a hard time believing it myself. I was afraid any explanation I tried to make would only scare you. Can you ever forgive me?"

"Mrs. Snyder, there's nothing to forgive." Bethany could hardly get the words out before she found herself sobbing on Mrs. Snyder's shoulder.

Eventually pulling herself back, Bethany took a tissue from the box Joe had gotten for them and dried her eyes. "Don't you see? We were meant to find each other. My mother knew I would need a family, and she wanted it to be you."

There was a slight pause before Joe spoke up. "When Nicholas told us about your mother and that she was considering giving you up for adoption, we thought that was our answer to a having a family after losing Sarah."

"Especially after the day your mother visited the clothes closet, and she let me hold you while trying on your coat. I remember studying every feature of your face as I did," Mrs. Snyder added. "The ones I still see."

Bethany's eyes widened. "You actually held me?"

Mrs. Snyder sucked in a deep breath and nodded. "And then we learned she changed her mind. But as heartbreaking as it was, Bethany, don't think for a minute that we weren't happy for the both of you. It was obvious how much your mother loved you, she was just alone and frightened. Seeing how you've grown up only confirms she made the right decision."

"Any chance we were ever one of your percolator prayers?" Bethany sniffled, trying to lighten the moment.

For the first time since their conversation began, Mrs. Snyder managed to smile. "Every single day."

Bethany looked away in reflection. "So, this was actually the second time for me to have been stranded in Snow Valley in a snowstorm at Christmas. The first time was when my mother borrowed the coat, which is how the poem ended up inside one of the pockets."

Mrs. Snyder dried her eyes another time. "The coat fit her just as perfectly as it does you, but she decided not to keep it, returning it to the closet before she left town."

Bethany gave a soft chuckle, looking at Joe and Mrs. Snyder. "Do you know how impossible this all sounds? I wouldn't be surprised if my mother already knew Nicholas had passed away."

Joe finally smiled as well. "All I know is, it's been nothing short of a miracle having you here with us."

"Which only makes me wish even more that this Christmas would never end," Bethany lamented. "I don't want to go back to the city, but it seems I don't have a choice."

"What makes you think you don't have a choice?" Mrs. Snyder questioned softly.

Bethany was tentative to answer. "You've been so kind to let me stay in your home, but I wouldn't want to start imposing, and I don't have any prospects for a job here."

"Bethany Mason, you could never impose on us. You've brought new life into our hearts and this home. It's yours for as long as you like." Mrs. Snyder paused to glance at Joe. "But more important than that, is how much we want you to be happy. It has to be the right decision for you."

Joe looked at Bethany a bit sheepishly. "I know it wouldn't be anything like working for a designer handbag company, but Joe Jr., is wanting to spend more time at the café, wearing his chef hat, so I could use another assistant at the store."

"And Max really does need to find someone to take over Antiques and Such. Even if that someone wasn't you, I know you would have some good ideas to help him showcase the shop better," Mrs. Snyder added.

Bethany laughed. "I will have to give those ideas some serious thought. No matter what happens, though, there's no getting rid of me. There's nothing that will keep me from visiting you as much as possible. Nell has already said she would teach me how to work with leather." Then tipping her head, "Speaking of Nell, I hope there's a good turnout at the cafe."

"I was able to plow all the roads, so everyone who usually comes should be there…and maybe even a few extras," Joe responded with a wink.

Bethany sighed, not wanting to get her hopes up that Christopher would be one of those extras. If they were never anything else but friends, she at least wanted to thank him for finding the note and giving it to her. "It's going to be hard to wait until time to get ready, since we don't have any cooking to do."

"I happen to know a perfect solution for that." Mrs. Snyder walked over next to the television and pulled out a movie from the shelf below and held its cover for Bethany to see. "How about watching this one?"

"It's a Wonderful Life," Bethany read out loud, then grinned. "You're right, Mrs. Snyder, it is perfect."

Chapter Thirty-nine

By the time the movie ended, there was still enough time to get ready and arrive at the café early enough to help Charlene. While she wouldn't be wearing her dress again, Bethany still wanted to look nice. She fixed her hair different than the night before, but still using the crystal barrette Mrs. Snyder had given her. The whole time she was getting dressed and fixing her hair, however, she couldn't get her mind off of staying in Snow Valley. Watching the end of the movie only made the idea more tempting, the way the community rallied around George in the end. She knew the people of Snow Valley were the type to do the same thing.

Bethany supposed she could stay a little longer. She had more vacation days she needed to use before the kick-off of the new spring collection. Her mind was still mulling the possibilities when she walked out of her room, putting her coat and new gloves on. Glancing out the front window, she saw the snow had stopped, but she would never doubt, it could start again.

Mrs. Snyder walked in from the kitchen. "I think someone must be hungry, to be the first one ready."

Bethany swung her head around with a smile. "Starving actually. I can't wait until we can dig into the cheeseballs."

"Don't worry, there will be plenty more than those to eat. We spend the whole afternoon eating and playing games."

"Games? What kind?"

By then, Joe had joined them in the living room. "Take your pick. There's always plenty of cards and boardgames to choose from, plus the rousing game of trivia Joe Jr. puts together. Whichever team loses has to wash dishes."

"Don't tell anyone I'm not very good at it, so I'll have a chance to be on the winning team," Bethany confided.

Joe walked over to open the door for them to leave. "Your secret is safe with me, but I will say there's been times the winning team has started counting their chickens before they hatched."

There were already several cars in front of the café when they pulled up, making it appear others were just as hungry. They entered to greetings of "Merry Christmas," and the most delicious aromas Bethany had ever smelled. She was just hanging up her coat when Nell ran over to her.

"Follow me so I can give you your Christmas present."

"But Nell, I didn't get anything for you."

Nell was already bent over behind the counter taking something off the shelf. "You've given me more than you could possibly know. Once you open this, you'll see the gift is really for the both of us anyway."

"And don't be slower than dirt about it either," Charlene walked up from behind, teasing. "I had a feeling Nell was being extra sneaky about something lately."

Bethany eyed everyone watching her as Nell placed the wrapped gift in front of her. "I guess we should find out then." She removed the paper, then the lid. Her jaw dropped open as she looked into Nell's expectant face. "Nell! I don't even know what to say."

"Just say you don't mind that I took one of the designs from your sketchbook and added a few small flourishes of my own," her voice was riddled with hesitancy. "I wanted you to see what it would look like brought to life. You're a talented designer, Bethany."

Bethany threw her arms around her in a huge hug. "And you're the best friend a person could ever hope for. Thank you, Nell."

"Goodness girls. How long are you going to keep us in suspense?" Charlene appeared ready to burst.

Staring at the gift still inside the box, Bethany realized this was the answer to staying in Snow Valley she had been looking for. As long as Nell was willing to give the business a try, it was time they come up with a plan. She then lifted the purse out of the box for everyone to see. "You're looking at the first original handbag produced by Nell and me. I can only hope it's the first of many." Bethany caught Nell's affirming nod before looking at Joe and Mrs. Snyder.

"Does this mean you're considering staying?" Mrs. Snyder asked as if her next breath was hinging on the answer.

Bethany's mouth gave way to her broadest smile yet. "I'm home, Mrs. Snyder."

Mrs. Snyder grabbed hold of Bethany's hands. "You have no idea how much we wanted you to stay, but we didn't dare let ourselves hope."

"Well, you're stuck with me now," Bethany laughed. "And Joe its looks like I'll be needing that assistant job at the store. I'll talk to Max, too, about helping out at Antiques and Such, until we can get our business going."

"This is about the best Christmas I could have asked for," Charlene spoke up, dabbing the corners of her eyes with her apron.

Bethany watched Mrs. Snyder walk over to the friend who had helped shoulder the weight of her grief all these years, and give her a hug. "All the more reason to start celebrating."

Charlene took a deep breath and smiled at all the guests who had arrived. "Okay everyone, there's plenty of appetizers to start eating and games to play while I check on the turkey and all the fixings."

Bethany joined Nell in line for some of the cheeseball, first. "Nell, I'm so excited. Are we crazy for trying this?"

"I think we'd be crazy not to," Nell answered with a look of confidence. "But no matter what happens, we're going to have fun."

"Yes, we are," Bethany confirmed, making a toast with their crackers. "Will Eliot and his family be coming to dinner?"

Nell shook her head. "No, they had family come in from out of town, but he did say he would come by later today."

Bethany raised an eyebrow. "I see."

Nell was already blushing when she attempted to divert the conversation. "So, what game do you want to start playing?"

"Max and Kathryn look to be starting a game of Scrabble." Bethany led the way toward their table. "Mind if we join you?"

"As long as you're not afraid to play against a champion here," Max grinned, motioning toward Kathryn.

Bethany smiled. It had been years since she had played any of these games, but she remembered liking it when she did. They were close to finishing the first round when her sole attention was on the board and the letters she had left.

"Uh, Bethany..." Nell prompted.

"I'm hurrying. I just know I can make a word somewhere," Bethany responded, keeping her eyes focused on the board.

"How about the word *bell*," a voice said.

Bethany's head jerked up to see the three other people at the table, smiling at someone behind her. She already knew by the way her heart had begun pounding, who it was.

"Right there." Christopher's arm reached over her shoulder to show her. "You have the *b* and the other *l*."

Bethany turned her head around to see him, though he looked different somehow. The hardened edges of his demeanor had softened and his eyes were brighter. "You came."

"Of course," he responded as if there had never been any doubt he would. "May I talk with you a minute?"

It was then, Bethany realized how quiet the inside of the café had grown and wondered how they were possibly going to talk with any privacy.

"You two head on back to the kitchen where only the pies will hear you," Charlene motioned with her words.

Bethany stood from her chair, noticing all the rest of the smiling faces and an extra wink from Joe as they walked in that direction. Once they were through the swinging doors and past the ovens, she stopped to take a breath and turned around. "I need to say something first. I want you to know how grateful I am that you found the note from your father. He and your mother showed nothing but compassion and kindness to a complete stranger and her infant daughter."

Christopher held her gaze. "I always knew my parents never met a stranger. I understand that better now."

"I'm just glad I had a chance to tell you in person. Nell said she had invited you, but after you didn't want to stay for the chili supper last night, I figured you wouldn't come."

"Bethany, it wasn't because I didn't want to stay."

"Then why did you leave?"

The warmth of Christopher's eyes seemed to meld into hers as if they were creating their own alloy. "You'll have to close your eyes and hold out your hand to find out."

Bethany reluctantly left his gaze and did as he instructed, holding out her left hand and feeling something gently come to rest against her skin.

"You can open them now," he said.

Her eyelids slowly rose until she saw what was in the palm of her hand. It was the shiniest sleigh bell she had ever seen. Not only that, there was a different maker's mark engraved in the brass. Instead of the initials *NS* were *CS*. "You did it, Christopher! It's beautiful." She then jingled the bell. "Your father would be so proud of you."

Christopher looked at Bethany. "I couldn't have done it without you. If you hadn't come to Snow Valley, or been so persistent, or found the poem, none of this would have happened."

He paused a moment before continuing. "And I'm not only talking about making a sleigh bell. I could never see a future here, and now that's all I see. It's you, Bethany Mason, you're what I see."

Bethany's eyes were hopeful as she held her breath and searched his face. "Are you telling me what I think you are? That you've decided not to sell the property?"

Christopher answered her question with a grin. "After being reminded that things are often not appreciated until they're gone, and looking over the long history of Smiths in Snow Valley, how could I? There was something special here that made them want to stay, it just took me a while to figure out what it was. After making some adjustments to my real estate business, I plan on being here as often as I can. It's home, after all."

"Well, it just so happens I'm staying in Snow Valley, too. I've decided to assist Joe and Max while Nell and I create our own line of leather products." Bethany then shook her head, amazed at how her life had taken such an unexpected turn in such a short amount of time. She had thought her life was falling apart, when all this time it was really falling into place.

"Did I miss something?" Christopher asked, suddenly curious.

Bethany peered into the eyes of the man she had fallen in love with. "Not a thing, though we should probably get back out there before there's too much talk, and we won't want to miss the trivia game. Whichever team loses has to wash all the dishes."

Christopher laughed. "As long as you're by my side, I win either way."

And with a kiss Bethany glanced up, filled with the promise of a sleigh bell, and gratitude for her mother's final gift…one that would last her a lifetime.

Blizzard Stew

1 pound of ground beef
1 can (10 ounces) diced tomatoes and green chilies
2 cans (15 ounces each) ranch style beans, undrained
2 cans (10.5 ounces each) condensed minestrone soup
1 soup can of water
8 ounces American cheese, or other pasteurized cheese

Brown the ground beef in large pot over medium heat. Drain any fat. Add remaining ingredients. Simmer for 15-20 minutes, stirring until thoroughly heated and cheese has completely melted. Serve with any choice of warm bread or cornbread. Makes 4-6 servings.

If you enjoyed *A Sleigh Bell Promise*
read *Heartstrings* today!

Enjoy an Excerpt from
Heartstrings

Chapter One

Beads of perspiration trickled down Anna Holmes' forehead while she stood over the steaming containers of food, filling one plate after another. Only once did she stop long enough to wipe her face dry with the hem of her apron. It may have been the first day of autumn, but summer was refusing to give up its turn, transforming the kitchen at the Samaritan Center into a sauna instead.

"Hey, Miss Anna."

Anna looked up into the face that reminded her of soft, tanned leather and smiled. "Hi, Mr. Harmon, how is the new job going?"

"As long as it pays the bills and keeps Sugar happy then I'm happy," he chuckled.

Anna was puzzled by Mr. Harmon's answer. They had both been volunteering at the Samaritan Center for years now, and for some reason she assumed he lived alone. "I've never heard you talk about anyone named Sugar before."

Mr. Harmon flashed his warm but crooked grin. "Why, she's been my roommate ever since I heard her meowing at my door a few days ago. I didn't want her to be homeless like I once was."

Anna returned his grin despite the sting she felt when she heard the word homeless. "Sugar sounds like one lucky cat, but make sure you don't forget to take care of yourself first."

"Not to worry, Miss Anna. We take care of each other," he assured her with a long nod. "But look who's talking about taking care of yourself. You best take a break from that kitchen and cool off, or we'll soon be picking you up off the floor. Go on now, I'll take over."

Mr. Harmon was right. The heat was suffocating, and she wouldn't be of any help to anyone if she fainted. Leaving her apron on, Anna walked out the front door and found a small area against the building where there was an overhang of shade. She lifted her long auburn curls away from her neck then closed her eyes as a gentle breeze came to offer its small gift of relief.

"It looks like I came at the right time. Break time."

Anna's eyes flew open with a sudden rush of guilt for having left the kitchen. That was until she saw who was speaking to her.

"I'm E.C. Coleman, here to volunteer my services," he announced.

Anna already knew the name that went with the dark wavy hair and long eyelashes that never should have been wasted on a boy. She hesitated a moment then remembered the assignment their government teacher had made. Any student willing to participate in a community service project could earn extra credit. One of the choices he had listed was the Samaritan Center.

"You must be here to earn your bonus points," she said.

E. C. looked surprised. "Yeah, how did you know?"

Anna didn't take her eyes off of his while she answered, "Last hour government class, fourth row, sixth seat back."

"Sorry, I never noticed you were in there," he shrugged. "Isn't Mr. Jenkins great? All we have to do is show up, put in a few hours and we've got as good as an A."

Anna would never have expected E.C. Coleman to know she existed. He was on the football team and a member of the popular crowd. She wasn't. She was used to not being noticed. Even so, Anna wasn't about to let him think she was there only for a grade.

"I'm here every Wednesday afternoon and not because of any class. I need to get back to work now." She turned around to walk back inside, wishing he'd change his mind and go away.

E.C. followed behind her instead. "What is it I have to do?"

Anna wanted to tell him he didn't have to do anything, that the center didn't need his self-serving acts of charity. But it wasn't true. The number of volunteers had fallen over recent months, and they were in need of more help. "Sign in on the sheet by the door. I'll get you an apron and a pair of gloves."

E.C. put the apron on by himself, but was struggling to get the gloves stretched over his hands. "I can't get these things on. They're too small."

Anna was unmoved by his apparent frustration. "Sorry, they're one size fits all. Everyone has to wear them, it's the rules."

"In case you haven't noticed, my hands aren't like everyone else's," he spouted back.

She would have let him continue struggling on his own, but there were people waiting in line to be served, and she needed to relieve Mr. Harmon. "I'll help you this time."

Even after Anna discovered how much larger E.C.'s hands were, she was determined to make him wear them. "There, that wasn't so difficult," she finally said, basking in her private victory.

"Now, what?" he asked, still tugging at the gloves while walking with Anna to the food containers.

"Why don't you start by serving the green beans if you think you can handle it," she answered him.

E.C.'s only response was to pick up the large spoon and begin placing green beans onto the plates.

Anna stayed busy serving the mashed potatoes and meatloaf, but was able to catch an occasional glimpse of E.C. out of the corner of her eye. She didn't know much about him except that he was on the football team, and it was obvious how awkward he felt being there. His apron wasn't big enough to hide the stark contrast between his designer label clothes and those of the less fortunate they were handing meals to. Anna couldn't imagine he had any idea what it was like to need or want for anything.

"You could look up every once in a while and at least smile. Green beans can't be all that fascinating," Anna said after a while to break the silence between them.

"Excuse me. I didn't realize that was in the job description," E.C. replied coolly. "I thought I was just here to serve food."

Anna wished she had kept quiet. She turned away and fixed her eyes on the rows of tables filled with people eating what might be their only meal of the day. "I've been here long enough to learn that people are hungry for more than just food. Feeding their dignity is important, too."

"Well, since you seem to have had more practice at this, you can be their soul food while I take care of their stomachs," he said, ending with a smirk.

Anna started to tell him he had won the grand prize for being the rudest human being she had ever met, but then decided to save her breath. The people they were serving didn't fit into his privileged life style and neither did she. If E.C. Coleman knew about her past or where she lived, Anna was certain he would never speak to her again.

Relieved when it was time to stop serving, Anna's attention turned to removing the leftover food. That was until she heard the frenzied voice cry out from the dining room. "He's pointing at me again."

Anna didn't bother to offer E.C. an explanation. She ran from the kitchen to the table where a woman was on her feet, her eyes bulging with fear. Anna took the woman's hands and spoke gently. "It's all right Mrs. Harris, he's gone now. Go ahead and finish your dinner. I'll stay with you and make sure he doesn't come back."

A bewildered expression faded from the woman's face before she settled back in her chair and began eating again. Anna sat down in the empty chair next to her and glanced over at the serving window. E.C. was no longer in sight.

Once she was confident Mrs. Harris's delusion wouldn't return, Anna walked back into the kitchen where Mr. Harmon was stacking the dirty trays. "I guess the new volunteer already left?" she asked.

"Yes, ma'am, and he sure was in a hurry. As soon as I mentioned what an angel you were around here, he was gone in a flash," Mr. Harmon answered then shook his head. "You ought to have seen him getting those gloves off though."

Picturing E.C. battle the gloves for a second time made Anna laugh. She suspected he had already changed his mind about volunteering for extra credit. She wasn't at all surprised he was gone. She was more surprised by how long he stayed.

Anna grabbed a rag to wipe off the counters and wondered why Louisa hadn't joined them yet. She was usually in the kitchen by now, lathering and rinsing the dishes, while singing songs in a language no one at the center could understand. Anna worried that the housekeeping job had become too difficult for her, that the arthritis had gnarled her fingers too much. But Louisa would be the last one not to do her work or complain.

Maybe she had fallen asleep while she was resting Anna thought, trying not to be alarmed. She finished the counters then looked down the hallway connecting the kitchen to Louisa's room and saw the door was closed. Anna considered knocking then changed her mind. There was no reason to disturb her. Louisa would come out when she was ready.

Anna went to the closet and pulled out her backpack and violin, being careful not to bump the case. Its frayed and cracked edges made it as worn and fragile as the instrument inside. "This was my great grandfather's," she had proudly announced the first time she took it to her orchestra class. But Anna didn't need to hear the snickering that followed to know how inferior her violin was compared to the others.

The words from her orchestra teacher still haunted her, "I believe you have a lot of talent, Anna. When you're able to get a better violin and take lessons, I know you'll be a fine player."

A few weeks later, Anna's father was laid off from his job and her younger brother had to be taken to the emergency room because of a severe asthma attack. Her parents had yet to be able to afford either one. If it hadn't been for Louisa, she would never have dreamed a music scholarship to the university was possible.

Anna stepped out of the Samaritan Center and thought back to the afternoon she first met Louisa. She had gone to the center early that Wednesday to practice her music, unaware that a new housekeeper had been hired. As she struggled through a difficult passage, a stranger's voice broke through her concentration.

"You must let the violin sing."

Anna's head jerked around to see an old woman with stooped shoulders and a head of disheveled white curls staring at her with piercing intensity.

"You must let the violin sing," the woman repeated.

Startled by this woman who seemed to have appeared out of nowhere, Anna stammered an apology. "I…I'm sorry. I don't have the best violin."

The woman looked tired and frail, but there was a determined spark in her eyes. "Every violin has a voice. You come here for a lesson this time every week, and I will help you to find it."

Anna had been too stunned to question the woman's

peculiar accent or her knowledge of violins, much less what she was doing at the Samaritan Center. Curiosity drove her to arrive early again the next Wednesday where she found the woman sitting in a chair, waiting on her. Louisa had been teaching and guiding her ever since.

An unexpected swirl of cooler air wound around Anna's arms as she turned down the last block toward home. It produced a shiver as she held the handle to her violin case a little tighter. Maybe summer was going to let autumn have its chance after all. That's all Anna was hoping to have with her violin, just a chance.

From the Author

I feel nothing but blessed and thankful to be able to write stories I hope will inspire my readers. I'm especially grateful for Jennifer McMurrain and Brandy Walker and for the support of family and friends that continue to help make it possible. I love every one of you.

Craftsmanship is something I've always admired, both in its artistry and in the knowledge and skill it requires, either creating things or fixing them. I watched a craftsman cast a sleigh bell once and was fascinated by the time-honored tradition of the materials and the process. In the past, fastening sleigh bells to horses was a way to warn pedestrians of an approaching vehicle, since sleighs were unable to stop quickly. Another use for them was to signal when someone important was coming. While those reasons aren't as necessary anymore, the sound of sleigh bells still evokes the feelings of anticipation and wonder, the same ones we feel at Christmas.

Not unlike the sleigh bell in this story, one of the most memorable Christmas gifts I received growing up was a pocket watch chain that belonged to my father. He had passed away before I was old enough to have any memory of him, yet my mother made sure I was given something of his at the appropriate age that I would always cherish, and I do. Years later, it was his violin she had kept that became the inspiration for my first Legacy Novel, *Heartstrings*.

May all of you be filled with the spirit of the season, and may its gifts, wrapped and unwrapped, bring you joy.

About the Author

Marilyn Boone is the award-winning author of *Heartstrings*, her first Legacy Novel which won the category for Best Juvenile Book at the Oklahoma Writers' Federation Inc. annual conference. She is a graduate of the University of Tulsa with a bachelor's degree in elementary education and has also won awards for her short stories, poetry, and inspirational articles. When not writing, Marilyn enjoys many other creative and musical activities that include baking and playing her hammered dulcimer.

A Sleigh Bell Promise is the first Heart of Christmas Novel, a stand-alone series of inspirational romance novels.

Other Works by Marilyn Boone

Legacy Novels
Heartstrings
Becoming Rose
Lillian's Locket

Book Contributor
Chicken Soup for the Soul: Reboot Your Life

Magazine Contributor
Guideposts: Angels on Earth

Anthologies and Collaborations
Celebrating Christmas: An Anthology of Tales, Tips, and Truths about Christmas
A Weekend with Effie
Seasons Remembered
Seasons of Life
Seasons to Celebrate
Tea Cozies and Terabytes

Visit her on her website
http:/www.marilynboone.com

Made in the USA
Coppell, TX
14 September 2024

37308115R00163